NOMADIC PRESS

OAKLAND

111 FAIRMONT AVENUE
OAKLAND, CA 94611

BROOKLYN

475 KENT AVENUE #302
BROOKLYN, NY 11249

WWW.NOMADICPRESS.ORG

MASTHEAD

FOUNDING PUBLISHER
J. K. FOWLER

ASSOCIATE EDITOR
MICHAELA MULLIN

EDITOR
NINA SACCO

DESIGN
JEVOHN TYLER NEWSOME

INVITATIONS

Nomadic Press wholeheartedly accepts invitations to read your work during our open reading period every year. To learn more or to extend an invitation, please visit: www.nomadicpress.org/invitations

DISTRIBUTION

Orders by teachers, libraries, trade bookstores, or wholesalers:

Nomadic Press Distribution
orders@nomadicpress.org
(510) 500-5162

Small Press Distribution
spd@spdbooks.org
(510) 524-1668 / (800) 869-7553

Library of Congress Cataloging-in-Publication Data

Title: *We Grew Here*
p. cm.
Summary: From the depths of Oakland's rocky soil, fertile ground once rich with soul and prowled by Panthers, comes this defiant mantra of rhyme and reason. In the interconnected stories comprising *We Grew Here*, one journeys through the deep-rooted, diverse communities of this colorful Bayside city of trendsetters and go-getters. Amid the timely battle for The Town's future, transplants and locals collide for a prime space to call home. The cunning guides on this adventure-from-the-headlines are childhood friends, and Oakland Greeks, Pete and Alex—hustling in pursuit of the artist's life. Rife with vibrant prose and dialogue true to the mystique of "Oakland cool," We Grew Here is a commanding novel-in-stories from hometown author, Apollo Papafrangou.

[1. Fiction. 2. Fiction/Short Stories. 3. Greek. 4. American General.] I. III. Title.

LIBRARY OF CONGRESS CONTROL NUMBER: 2021945291

ISBN: 9781955239110

WE

GREW

HERE

Apollo Papafrangou

WE
GREW
HERE

Apollo Papafrangou

**NOMADIC
PRESS**

contents

foreword
introduction

reading guide

foreword

I first met Apollo Papafrangou in 1993 when he was thirteen years old. I had received a letter from him, written on school binder paper and forwarded to me by Farrar, Straus & Giroux, publisher of my novel, *Way Past Cool*, saying he'd read all my books, liked them, and wanted to be a writer. I get many letters from people of all ages, but there was a seriousness and sophistication in Apollo's that stood out from most others; something, perhaps, only a writer would recognize. He'd included a story he'd written—also on binder paper—and it was clear this young man not only had real writing talent but was already skilled at putting it to use. He asked if we could meet, and we arranged to hook up the next day at Marcus Books here in Oakland. He arrived escorted by his mother, an art teacher at a small private school in Berkeley, which Apollo attended, a polite and very articulate young man.

As Apollo continued developing new writing, all I could do was offer encouragement—the determination, dedication and self-discipline were entirely up to him—as well as first buying him a used typewriter and then, as it became evident he was serious about his writing, a word-processor.

Then, real-time success came to Apollo when one of his stories, "Four Wolves And A Panther," was accepted for publication by the prestigious San Francisco literary magazine, *ZYZZYVA*. This story was part of a collection he was working on about Oakland kids, titled *Concrete Candy*, which was purchased for publication a few months later by Anchor Books/Doubleday. *Concrete Candy* was also published in Denmark and France, making Apollo an internationally-published author at age 16.

Apollo's next manuscript was a dystopian novel titled *The Fence*, set

in the (then) near future of the early 21st century. The manuscript was optioned by HBO for a feature-length film in 2000 and remained in option until 2004 when the events of 9/11 (likely) rendered it too politically-incorrect—and perhaps too uncomfortably realistic—for the time. Still, a manuscript being optioned for film is a dream of many long-established writers, and one that will only come true for a few.

Apollo later attended Mills College where he earned an MFA in Creative Writing and went on to develop his graduate thesis project into his debut novel *Wings of Wax*, published in 2016 by Olive Leaf Editions, a vivid story about an estranged father and son seeking to reconnect across the waters and cultural divides separating Oakland and Greece.

In this latest work, *We Grew Here*, Apollo Papafrangou further bridges those places he knows so well via a keen sense of place and time, guiding us through the textured ethos of today's Oakland in all its diverse dynamics.

Jess Mowry
author of *Way Past Cool*

introduction

We Grew Here.

We locals are fiercely proud of our homegrown roots. Sure, our parents or grandparents may have ultimately come from somewhere else, but we arrived long before Oakland, CA, was the place to be. That fierce pride is at the heart of *We Grew Here*. It's a love letter to the Town from someone who has always called it home; an attempt at a time capsule capturing a charged, tumultuous time in Oakland's recent history.

Around 2013–14, this book began with the tiniest bud of an idea as change was blooming in my hometown. While the seeds of Oakland's gentrification were planted years earlier, businesses sprouted up faster than ever, crowding out old establishments with the stubborn determination of weeds pushing through pavement cracks.

I, like most locals, felt powerless to rise above the vines of change—some of it good, some bad. But, being a writer, I could at least document the transformation. On the concept of Oakland's inner turmoil, I had a story idea. Then another. Before long, I realized these new stories tackled similar themes, and I started including recurrent characters. A group of Greek-Americans in their twenties with dreams of making it as artists were based, in some sense, on myself as an "Oakland Greek." I also included a supporting cast of characters who, in reflecting the storied diversity of our city, were varied in their ethnicity and culture. I hope the stories and characters offer words of welcome to new arrivals, and phrases that resonate with fellow locals. If you flew here, and we grew here, maybe in reading this novel we can turn a page toward growing together.

Apollo Papafrangou
June 4, 2021

SUMMER
ΚΑΛΟΚΑΙΡΙ
2013

kissing
game

In the echoes of some great cosmic giggle, within one day of each other Alex Kouros and Pete Saropoulos were dumped by their girlfriends. Almost as if the women, through a last show of mercy, conspired to let them loose over a twenty-four-hour period in a back-handed gesture of kindness.

"Maybe they did us a favor," Alex said, sauntering alongside Pete as they approached the late-night burger joint serving the Oakland side of Telegraph Avenue, that stretch of shabby, scissor-iron security gates and pristine grand-opening banners waiting to be snipped. On this Saturday evening, they had just left the bar hosting an open-mic poetry reading. Before an audience of head-nodding twenty-somethings and old-school beat poet types, Alex had recited a new piece inspired by his recent heartache in which he'd utilized the phrase *memories to masturbate* by a half-dozen times. "Look at it like this," he continued, "if I was single while you were still in a relationship, or vice-versa, I'd probably be a little envious. This way, we equally feel like shit, and so everything's cool."

Pete shoved his hands in his jean pockets.

"Who knows, brother," said Alex, "this might be the motivation we need to really get out here on the grind."

The grind. Alex's favorite phrase—both a noun and verb that he Mad-Libbed into nearly every conversation since he and Pete had first met as third graders during a cookout at the Saropoulos residence. By way of the grind he would piece together the Ultimate Hustle. In part inspired by Pete's creative talents, Alex fashioned himself a graffiti artist, a budding chef, and most recently a poet—just to name a few of his enterprises—in effort to gain public recognition and a non-traditional paycheck.

"Y'know, that was Rachel's reason for ending things," Alex remarked, leaned against the counter in anticipation of his burger. "She said I was 'too *diluted*,' whatever that even means. And she claimed it was too hard to keep up with me. Can you believe that? She resents my ambition. Not my fault I see opportunity most everywhere I go. Look at all this space here," he said, indicating the eatery's front wall. "This is practically *begging* to hold some art. You should ask the owner to let you paint a mural."

Pete smirked. "With the typical clientele this spot pulls in, any mural will be tagged in no time."

Alex shook his head. "Ever the pessimist."

A bum shuffled over to gaze at them with eyes like street lamps. Alex dropped a crumpled dollar into his palm. The duo watched the man stagger away.

"My girl got on me for a *lack* of ambition," Pete said. "Go figure."

"Well, she has a point there," Alex said, receiving his food through the delivery slot.

Pete shrugged, but stayed quiet.

"Sure, we're hurting over the loss of our women now, but women will … hey! *That's* what we should do."

"What?" Pete asked.

"Open a kissing booth."

Pete laughed.

Alex only shrugged. "You know, like the ones from those old-time carnivals. The way it works—"

"I *know* what a kissing booth is, *malaka*," Pete cut in, "and it's got to be your dumbest idea yet."

Alex didn't even blink. "Everybody thinks the best ideas are the dumbest until they're proven wrong. I'm sure even the guy who thought up the first corner burger stand had friends who tried to discourage him."

Pete snagged his own food through the slot. "Obviously, selling burgers and selling kisses is an entirely different game."

"We won't be selling kisses. I mean, we will be, technically, but really we're going to sell an *experience*. A fun and lighthearted one that fits in great with the overflow from the First Fridays art scene downtown. Think about it. First Friday already features galleries, street musicians, food vendors. It brings out couples on the stroll, and singles wanting to flirt. A kissing booth is totally original! Picture this intro: 'Step right up, ladies, a small donation will earn you a smooch from your choice of two—count 'em—two dashing, enterprising Greek gents!'"

"I've always admired your ambition, but I have to agree with Rachel that it's out of hand. What's the *real* reason behind this idea?"

Alex shrugged. "A great way to meet women."

Pete laughed again. "Might've known! Man, I should've never shown you that girly mag when we were kids. I created a monster."

Alex laughed, too. "I'll need your help with this."

"No way," said Pete. "I'm not getting involved."

"It won't be a huge commitment. Think of it as a new art project."

Pete took a deep breath.

A week later, they stood in Alex's driveway, hands-on-hips, panting in the twilight, their ragged work clothes dusted with wood debris. Over the course of the afternoon, their carpentry project yielded a fairly sizable structure: three-sided with a small front counter not unlike the one gracing the Telegraph burger joint. In fact, their booth might have been seen as the burger stand in miniature.

Pete pointed out that in an era of hyper political-correctness, the attraction might be an unwelcome reminder of traditional kissing booths in which objectified women had offered their "prized" lips to anyone with cash to blow.

"Don't stress so much, dude," Alex said as they carried the booth into the garage, "anyone with a sense of humor will see it's all in good fun. Besides, we're the only ones being objectified."

"You're probably right," Pete conceded. "But what about hygiene? There's a thousand diseases you can get from swapping saliva with strangers."

Alex chuckled. "Relax, okay? You can tell the ladies to only kiss you on the cheek, and we'll have somebody screen them for herpes blisters and all. Best case scenario, we lock lips with our future girlfriends. Worst case, I make a name for myself as 'The Kissing Booth Guy,' and you build a new audience for your paintings."

"How do you figure?"

They set the booth down in a corner of the garage, contemplating the structure in silence before Alex finally answered, "You're going to do a mural on this thing."

Pete shrugged. "If you say so."

Back in the driveway the next evening, Alex retreated a few paces to admire the results of his friend's craftsmanship as Pete, armed with a spray can, added the finishing touches to his mural. On one side of the booth a shapely Aphrodite bathed in Mediterranean waters, while on the other side a stylized version of Cupid; the Roman god's lips puckered in anticipation of a kiss.

"Now, that wasn't so bad, was it?" asked Alex.

Pete set down the spray can and wiped his brow. "Easy for you to say. So, what's next?"

"How about a couple beers on me? We sip some cold ones and discuss the stakeout."

The following First Friday night, Alex and Pete took in the art walk festivities among the weathered brick along 19th Street and Telegraph Avenue. In straying from the juxtaposed crowd of pink-haired, heavily-tattooed rocker chicks, white guys sporting skinny jeans and handle-bar mustaches, and young black men in Oakland A's gear, they paused in front of the Fox Theater. A brief interval if only for the sake of basking in the glow of its giant neon ideogram spelling 'OAKLAND,' the letters pink as a panther's tongue. Alex stayed off to the side, listening to the stanky, low-bottom bass and jabbing horn riffs of a multiethnic funk band like a jamming rainbow. Meanwhile, Pete approached a fellow visual artist showcasing his vaguely psychedelic paintings. Alex couldn't hear the discussion, but Pete kept smiling and making wide, sweeping gestures with his hands.

"What was that about?" Alex asked.

Hands in his pockets, Pete resumed his sheepish demeanor as he said, "Guy's apparently represented by a gallery over on Twenty-seventh. I described my work and he said it might be a good fit."

"There you go! Glad my influence is rubbing off."

Pete made a face. "There you go taking all the credit." Before Alex could protest, Pete added, "I know, I know, 'relax.' Anyway, have you seen an ideal spot for the kissing booth yet?"

"No, this area's too crowded. I'm thinking we should cruise one of the streets further up and over."

They strolled past the hollows of Broadway's spent blue collar vein. More musicians, and even a fire-eater on stilts, performed in front of the car dealerships and detail shops along Auto Row. Alex pointed out a man in the crowd, a bushy-bearded, twenty-something wearing suspenders and cradling a paper bag, the top of which failed to fully conceal a beer can.

"Check this guy," remarked Alex with a chuckle. "It's like he walked into a costume shop and said, 'Accessorize me for hipster-dom.' Hey, buddy," Alex shouted, "Welcome to Oakland. We grew here, you just flew here." The hipster didn't look their way as they turned down Twenty-fifth, a shabby side street of barbed-wire fences and brick warehouses-turned-art galleries. A food truck selling gourmet Dominican cuisine idled at the curb, and they joined the line of patrons.

"This little spot here," Alex said, indicating the square of sidewalk in front of the truck, "is perfect for our booth! Good amount of foot traffic on this block. We'll attract a lot of people coming in and out of the galleries or stopping by the food truck. Speaking of, that'll be the next big project..."

"What?" asked Pete.

"Getting a food truck!"

"One hustle at a time, huh?"

Alex shrugged. "Always stay two steps ahead. Shit, *don't* look now, but I think that's Michelle over there. I said don't look!"

Blessed with an Oakland booty indeed, the woman swayed her hips in full knowledge that their circumference could damn near span the entire Bay Bridge. Pete sucked a breath through clenched teeth.

"Hey, boys," Michelle said, brushing a lock of dark hair behind her ear. "Enjoying the evening?"

"Definitely," said Alex, giving Pete a subtle jab in the ribs.

"Nice seeing you, Michelle, but we gotta run," Pete said at last.

Michelle smirked. "What, you got an actual job? Yeah, right."

"*Actually*," Pete replied, "I don't want to keep our dates waiting, y'know?"

Alex cleared his throat. "You handled that well."

Pete glared into the distance, doing his best to overlook the bounce in Michelle's goodbye. "When we open the booth," he said, "I give out the first kiss."

Despite the anticipated flow of foot traffic on this First Friday, not one woman had approached their booth. Sure, they had gained plenty of finger-points, whispers, and curious glances, but no one seemed curious enough to investigate. No one except a grinning man in a feather boa who had marched up to drop two dollars in the jar before giving both Alex and Pete a smooch on the cheek. "I can't figure it out," Alex finally said, watching yet another woman approach only to backtrack. "I mean, we're good looking guys, right? And I know not *all* these ladies have boyfriends. Even if they do, what's the harm in a little kiss for charity's sake?"

"Maybe a dollar was too high a price?"

Alex smiled. "Gee, don't sell yourself short or anything."

Pete chuckled. "Okay, they could just be shy. Maybe we're intimidating. It's hard to just go up and kiss someone you don't know."

"Really? People do it in bars all the time. Many a relationship has begun over a random kiss."

"Maybe the booze hasn't taken effect yet."

"Yeah, the night is young."

"For what it's worth," Pete said, "I still think this partition was a bad call. We probably look like bank tellers or something."

"With your sketchpad you look more like a—"

"Hey, that gives me an idea," said Pete.

Alex made a face. "That's *my* line."

"Just trust me."

Before Alex could make sense of the happenings, Pete, armed with his pad, stepped out from behind the booth. In big, bold letters he wrote:

'HAVE YOUR PORTRAIT DRAWN BY A PROFESSIONAL ARTIST. COSTS ONLY 1 DOLLAR AND A KISS!'

By the time the sun fully descended, the line of women at the kissing booth surpassed the line for the ultra-popular Dominican food truck. Whether photo selfie or an artist's portrait, millennials proved unable to resist their own image. It didn't take long for Alex and Pete to develop an ideal system: Pete stood outside the booth jotting quick portraits of each "customer," and then let the women lean in to lock lips with Alex.

Eventually, Alex playfully complained of a sore jaw, his lips and cheeks smeared rogue. After another two hours, they temporarily closed the booth to enjoy refreshments while tallying their profit overflow.

"I'll admit the 'artist' angle worked even better than the 'handsome Greek' one," said Alex.

Pete shrugged. "It's an artsy crowd. You make a real connection with any of the ladies?"

"I may have, as a matter of fact. And more than a few asked why you weren't back behind the booth, too."

"Maybe I'll give it a try next round."

Alex smiled. "And you'll forget about Michelle in no time."

"Already have."

"That's the right attitude," said Alex. "You've got more of the entre-preneurial spirit than you give yourself credit for, brother."

"I'm an Oakland Greek, what more can I say?"

The duo shared a laugh beneath a moon full and bright.

the Jumping acorn

Ten in total, arranged in a row, black and white, on the kitchen table, the kind of Apples that don't grow on trees. Alex Kouros watched the fruits of his labor blossom one-by-one; smart-phones smartened. Unhinged padlocks appeared on their screens, the devices now free to be used on any network in any place, and all thanks to his nimble handiwork. With open palms, he drummed a victory roll, and then checked the clock. Quarter-after-eight. The morning air carried the scent of exhaust as commuters twitched toward jobs downtown or across the Bay Bridge. Between sips of coffee and bites of buttered toast, Alex opened his laptop.

The week prior, Alex launched his site for True Oaktown Tours. A few days after, he had booked his first client: a slim, young guy from Portland, Oregon who called himself Bean and had the names of several yoga poses tattooed along his veiny forearms. By the time they had reached International Boulevard (still East 14th to those born-and-bred) in Alex's car, blasting golden-era Ant Banks through the stereo speakers, Bean had already incorporated the word "hella" into his vocabulary (using the term *hella* times over a couple-hour span). He had also asked Alex for details about the long defunct Festival at the Lake, and even begged him, in complete sincerity, to "ghost-ride the whip down the strip." A successful outing, in Alex's mind.

Alex logged into his E-mail. *THROUGH LOCAL EYES?* bellowed a subject line, a query from "Tiffany," friend of Bean, who had praised Alex's "homegrown vision."

Tiffany hoped for a meet-up that afternoon, so Alex suggested one-thirty at Rockridge BART. Next, he checked his site for a fresh take on the new photo. His friend Daphne, her dark eyes shimmering while her plum lipsticked-mouth formed that customary, sly half-smile, had said, "With those sharp cheekbones and piercing eyes like some Grecian hero, a hint of mystery in that gaze of yours. Jason of the Argonauts, reincarnate. Welcome aboard, ladies and, who knows, you might even attract a few gents."

Alex had shrugged. "As long as they're paying customers."

Daphne had asked, "So, this whole gig isn't just a sly way to up your chances of meeting someone?"

"We both know a relationship is the last thing I'm looking for."

Daphne's smile curled into a smirk. "You're still mad you couldn't hustle your way into my heart, hustler."

"Aw, Daphne . . ."

She chuckled. "Just tell me how I can help spread the word."

Tinkering with the phones again, Alex anticipated the door knock and rose from his chair. Through the years Yiayia had hinted at the hereditary nature of precognition. Alex had been content, as he'd grown older, to simply label it hustler's intuition.

A handful of people stood on his porch, among them his old friend, bartender Mike Lagounis. Alex ushered them into the kitchen and distributed a quintet of phones, watching as their owners tapped buttons, faces lighting up like the screens.

"So, we can roam free now?" Mike asked.

"No problem," Alex replied.

"And it's fifty even, yeah?"

"Just forty for you guys. Better deal than anywhere else. Do me a favor and spread the word about my new gig, True Oaktown Tours."

Alex stashed his earnings in a closeted Nike box. Two hundred bucks for three hours' work. Not bad at all.

He checked the time, and then laid a towel across the living room carpet, set a chair in the center, and donned an apron before getting his clippers from the bathroom. Again, he went to the door prior to hearing a knock. His father Dino, a man everyone claimed was a dead-ringer for a post-*Full House* John Stamos, stood on the porch with arms spread, wearing his usual rakish grin. "Ah, my boy!" he boomed in his Greek accent, "How are you?"

"I'm good, Dad. Nice to see you. Come in."

Dino glanced over his shoulder as his friend and next door neighbor, Mr. Petrakis, galloped up the steps like a white-whiskered ram trailed by a boy of six or seven. "*Ela, megaleh.*"

"Hi, Mr. Petrakis." Alex arranged his couch so that the elderly man and young boy could have a seat.

"Been a while since I last saw you at church, *palikari.*"

"Busy," said Alex.

Dino frowned a little. "With what, no one knows."

Alex went to the kitchen and poured a trio of lemonades.

Dino made a sour face.

Mr. Petrakis said, "I don't think you've met my grandson, Marko." Then, addressing the boy, "*Pes yiasou.*"

Marko, with a sheepdog mop of sable hair, waved before taking a gulp from his glass.

"*Yiasou*, Marko," said Alex. "So, you the one getting a haircut?"

"He is indeed," Mr. Petrakis answered.

Alex indicated the chair with the towel underneath. "What would you like, little man?"

Marko obediently seated himself, but Mr. Petrakis spoke for him again.

"A nice trim all around."

After draping a cape over Marko, Alex combed the boy's hair back. He ran a segment through his fingertips until the ends came poking out, and then snipped them with shears.

Dino leaned to Mr. Petrakis, but spoke loud enough for Alex to hear, "He has many talents, huh? I tried to tell him to go to barber school, but he don't listen."

Alex, keeping his eyes on Marko's head, replied, "You know how much barber college costs, Dad?"

"Your mother and I have money saved . . ."

Slice, slice.

"I don't want to make someone else rich."

"So, open your own place."

Slice, slice.

"I've got other interests," said Alex.

Dino sighed, and addressed Mr. Petrakis. "You see? Always the same answer, this one. *Malakia.*"

Slice, slice.

Spreading his palms, and turning to his son, Dino said, "You twenty-five now. Time to pick one interest and stick with it."

"Yeah, yeah, 'one job, one hair style, one woman,'" Alex countered, pausing with the scissors poised like the glinting beak of some hungry bird. Marko, seeming to sense potential danger, squirmed in his chair. "You always told me to be original and work for myself."

"You are right, but remember the key word is *work*. When I arrived from Greece with your mother, you think I didn't have many dreams? But I knew I had to support a family, so I chose to paint houses as I had done alongside my brothers back in the *horyo*. One thing. I worked a while for someone else, then took over the business, and made good money. That's the way it's done."

Slice, slice.

"Maybe so, Dad, but growing up I always heard the downside. The aching back, the tired knees. I'm not going to end up like that."

Dino frowned. "Like *what*? Like me, like your father?"

"Dad, that's not what I meant. Why not just be happy that I'm already making enough money to afford my own apartment in my hometown?"

"Some say," Mr. Petrakis began, "that to share your plans provides the same satisfaction as completing them. Good entrepreneurs have their eyes on many goals, so it's also often said."

Dino's frown deeped. "Who says? No-good bums?"

Mr. Petrakis spread his palms as if in truce. "I'm just another immigrant who opened one humble restaurant that in the end couldn't keep up with the tastes of Oakland newcomers. So, what do I know?"

Alex smiled at Mr. Petrakis, and then looked down at Markos, the boy's aproned chest scattered with hair, and decided he was done. He handed the child a mirror. "What do you think?"

"Quite refined, thank you very much," said Marko.

Alex cocked his head.

"The child reads a lot," Mr. Petrakis said with a shrug.

"Oh, yeah? You like poetry, Marko? On my shelf I've got a hella nice anthology of Oakland poets you can borrow. You feel them, you'll feel what I write."

Marko smiled wide. "I like to write, too. Are your poems in the book?"

"No," Alex said with reluctance. "But yours might be in the next one, buddy."

"What will I owe you for the cut?"

"Fifteen dollars, Mister Petrakis."

"That's how it's done," said Dino.

Alone again, Alex added the cash to his shoebox before tossing the towel in the hamper and vacuuming the carpet. His father's advice colored his thoughts like the man's paintbrushes had once coated walls.

His cell twanged a *bouzoukia* ringtone. "Daphne. Little early for a booty call, isn't it?" Across the connection, he could practically hear her eyes roll.

"Don't flatter yourself, big guy."

Alex chuckled. "How's it going?"

"Wondering if you've got the goods."

"Said I'd alert you to the ready batch."

"I know, but I just couldn't wait."

"Fiending for the flavor? Well, you're in luck. It's time to bag up."

"Great. See you in a few."

From the fridge Alex withdrew last night's pan of *spanakopita* and sliced the savory pastry into twenty-five squares, all spoken for at seven dollars a pop. Another one-hundred-seventy-five to fatten his shoebox.

He finished washing the pan and again sensed someone at the door.

"How do you do that?" Daphne asked, out on the porch, hand poised to knock.

"*Horyo* magic."

"But you were born here in Oakland."

"And, therefore, the hustle was born in me."

"Anyway," Daphne said, stepping inside and finding a spot on the couch, "where's my fix?"

Alex went to the kitchen and returned with a plate.

"Oh, yes," Daphne said, "this is the truth right here. Seven, right?"

Alex pocketed the money. "My lucky number."

Daphne took a crackling bite into the flaky *phylo* crust, its spinach-and-feta filling oozing out the edges. "Seriously, this is some of the best I've tasted. Almost as delicious as when Pete's mom makes it. You should open a food truck or something."

"I'm way ahead of you."

"On my coffee run, I chatted up a couple hipster-types and mentioned your new tour."

Alex smiled. "Thanks."

"Least I could do. The gig was kind of my idea, right?"

Alex recalled a recent First Friday art walk downtown, when he and Daphne had watched a young blonde couple clad in "I HEART OAKLAND" shirts, which like similar garments all over the world, were rarely worn by locals. The pair had ambled hand-in-hand toward some chic, new closet-sized taqueria that replaced a similar spot once run by actual Mexicans. Daphne had remarked, "I almost feel sorry for these people. Can you be mad at them? It's like getting angry with blind folks for walking into stores and knocking down displays."

"Yeah, a lot of these transplants are just wandering around looking for an authentic experience without seeing what's in front of them."

"They claim they're hungry for 'realness,'" Daphne said, "so why shouldn't a *real* native provide it?"

Alex had snapped his fingers. "Like through some kind of tour, right? Of all the real, old-school places."

Now, Alex handed Daphne a square of foil for her spanakopita. "Sorry, I gotta go. My services have been summoned."

Daphne smiled. "By all means. I'm never one to get between a man and his mission."

During their email exchanges, Tiffany had offered only a vague description of herself, and still, upon reaching the crosswalk opposite the BART station, Alex spotted her. In fact, he spotted many Tiffanys. On that luminous afternoon the sidewalk swarmed with them. Sure, their faces differed, but they all flaunted only slight variations of the same hairstyle and attire: short, boyish coiffures—half-shaved heads *ala* Miley Cyrus; faux-hawks meticulously rendered to appear non-meticulous; bowler hats or scruffy beanies balanced on the crowns of their heads. Faster and faster, the neighborhood, like so many others in the city, seemed to be transforming into a living layout for *Vice* magazine.

Alex's Tiffany smiled and waved.

"Hope you weren't waiting long," said Alex, reaching the curb.

Up close, Tiffany's smile revealed teeth like those cellophane-wrapped Chiclets given out at Alex's favorite taqueria that was no more. "Actually, I got here early so I could peruse that market across the street," she said. "When I first moved here, over on the Eastside, I was so frustrated that it seemed like a food wasteland, y'know? Just *nothing* in terms of restaurants, and *forget* grabbing a decent latte in the morning. But then I decided to bring myself down to earth. I actually *enjoy* getting my coffee from the mini-mart now. Feels like I'm starting to rub elbows with the natives, and it's kind of awesome. That's something I want to do a lot more, hence my contacting you. How long have you lived in this part of town? Seems like it's a place to be in terms of bars and restaurants and shopping."

"I grew up close by. Believe it or not, the area used to be

working class."

"I can't imagine."

"When I was a kid the blue collars had already started to fade, but a few traces remain if you know where to look."

Tiffany smiled once more. "Let's start the tour?"

Alex led the way along bustling College Avenue with its casual restaurants and vintage clothing boutiques, indicating them with a flippant hand. "The people next door used to say there was nothing here when they'd first arrived in the '70's. Maybe the one bar there, and another a few blocks up, and the burrito place. That was about it."

"Is that when the 'gentrifiers' first arrived?" Tiffany asked, ironically.

Alex shrugged. "Maybe so, but they belonged to those generations who came before the city was a hotspot. So, why did you come here?"

Tiffany pulled her gaze from the trance of shop windows. "I'd just gotten out of an abusive relationship. He put my head through a window."

Alex raised his eyebrows. "I'm sorry."

"Thank you." Tiffany paused to indicate her scalp. Earlier, in his dismissive scan of her hipster appearance, Alex had failed to notice the inch long scar etched across the side of her scalp. "I keep my hair short as, like, a badge of what I've overcome."

Alex looked away.

"Sorry," said Tiffany, "I know that was a lot. Anyhow, I'd had enough of Wisconsin, enough of the Midwest. The Left Coast is, like, really in line with my politics, y'know? Lately I've been itching to get behind a new cause. But I don't get why, when I cruise the Art Murmurs, the natives shout shit like, 'We grew here, you flew here!' I mean, I can't change where I was born or raised."

Alex shrugged. "Maybe they don't like being referred to as 'natives?'"

Tiffany blinked. "But your website bio emphasizes you're an 'Oakland native.'"

"True. A native of Oakland. 'Native' by itself kinda sounds . . . anyway, I think us locals are just amused that our city has become the hip, new destination when for so many years no one came through unless they had to."

"Maybe it was all the black-on-black crime?" Tiffany suggested, then added, "Of course I don't see color."

"Of course not," Alex muttered.

They continued up the block, and Alex watched a Budweiser semi pull to the curb outside the liquor store, brakes sighing as the driver parked and climbed down from the cab to roll open the trailer and load his dolly. He paused for a businesswoman strutting by in her fog-colored get-up. They swapped smiles. "So, what do you do?"

"For work, you mean?"

Alex nodded. "Do hipsters just click their Doc Martens and make money appear?"

"Sorry?"

"Nothing."

"I'm actually in between jobs. I saved some funds after my last gig working for a non-profit that fights for the rights of women who feel marginalized beyond the margins of the feminist movement."

Alex simply said, "Cool." As with previous tours, he had no real itinerary, finding it best to let the client's sensibilities determine the route. Since Tiffany seemed ignorant of the city's steely roots, he figured that would be a good angle to take today. Indicating the adjacent storefront with its window display of restoration-shined work boots and polished wingtips, he said, "This little shoe repair and leather shop might seem out of place beside all the boutiques, but it's been here since the forties. And this dive-of-a-bar? Since the thirties."

He escorted Tiffany across the street and up Kales Avenue where modest bungalows stood in understated hues—sandy yellows and granite grays—that seemed to reflect the down-to-earth sensibilities of the families within. Alex knew many of the "old" families who had been here prior to the wave of new middle class.

"Lovely homes," said Tiffany. "Any of them for sale?"

"Not that I know of. See the mustard-colored place three doors down? I went to elementary with Ms. Henderson's son, Travis. Now he lives clear out in Antioch. Can't even afford his own spot in his own city."

Tiffany blinked. "Whatever the reason, it's good for people to get away from home."

Alex felt a curse rising hot in his throat, but he choked it back down.

"I'd love to buy along this street," Tiffany went on, "but no doubt it's out of my price range. I just *love* houses. Especially vintage ones like these."

"Flip of your wrist," Alex muttered, "and there goes the neighborhood."

"What was that?"

Alex fought the impulse to roll his eyes. "I don't know about you," he said, "but I haven't eaten lunch yet. Low blood sugar lowers my bullshit tolerance. You hungry?"

"Lunch sounds great," Tiffany replied. "How about that Mexican place across from the BART station? We'll have to walk that way anyhow if we're going to grab my car for the rest of the tour."

"You mean where the old Chimes Market used to be," said Alex. "All the newbies go there. Mind if I suggest another place?"

Soon they were cruising downtown in Tiffany's Prius, and Alex pointed out a shiny new bar. "That spot used to be a hole-in-the-wall, Greek-owned diner. Mr. Petrakis catered to both lunch-breakers and partiers emerging from bars with two AM hunger pangs. High rents pushed him out, and now he just caters to his grandson."

They arrived at the Jumping Acorn, a little brick shack of a blues club near Jack London Square. Summoned by the southern-fried guitar licks twanging through the open door, Alex led Tiffany across the venue's murky interior, past its Hennessy-stained leather couches, and through a narrow doorway near the small stage. Allured by the scents of cumin and garlic, they entered a dining room equipped with only a quartet of clothed tables, and a counter space fronting a tiny, open kitchen. Alex seated Tiffany, then approached the counter, drumming his knuckles atop the chipped, seafoam-green Formica. Glancing over his shoulder, he caught Tiffany eyeing the walls decorated with autographed photos of the many celebrities who had visited the establishment: everyone from Mahershala Ali to Ricky Henderson.

A slim seventeen-year-old appeared; white button-down draped on his frame like a painter's smock rolled up at the sleeves to reveal Greek key pattern tattoos. He flashed a cherub's smile.

"Tommy boy," Alex said, shaking the youth's hand. "No school?"

Tom Eliopoulos shrugged. "Teachers meeting."

"And this is how you're spending your afternoon off?"

"Another day, another dollar. You know how it is."

"Damn, your brother's written whole songs about the hustle. 'No obstacle too tough, try your luck, get it any way you can, young buck.' That's my jam right there. I remember when Johnny first played it for me in the studio on Wood Street."

Alex glanced over his shoulder again to check on his client still ogling the wall portraits. "Tiffany, I'd like you to meet a friend of mine." When she joined him at the counter, Alex said, "Tiffany, this is Tom Eliopoulos. I'm sure he can share another perspective on growing up here."

Tom's pomaded hair, slicked back from his forehead, gleamed like polished obsidian beneath the overhead lamps.

"Wow," said Tiffany, "you look like one of the guys in those photos with a microphone."

Tom flashed his babyish simper. "That's my brother Johnny. Some people know his music, I guess."

Alex chuckled. "He's being modest. Johnny Eliopoulos performs all over town. He's got a great voice. Only a matter of time before he blows up nationally. He got his start in this club."

Tom smiled. "My family is tight with Mister Lawson."

"And I'm assuming with the last name 'Eliopoulos' you're also Greek, like Alex?"

Tom nodded.

"I don't guess there are many Greek soul singers," said Tiffany.

"That's everybody's first reaction," said Alex. "But they usually become believers once they hear the music."

Tiffany regarded the photos again. "This place is sort of like a landmark!"

"Indeed." Alex turned to Tom. "I'm taking Tiffany on a tour of the *real* Oakland."

"And what is that, exactly?" Tiffany asked.

"Hard to explain," said Tom. "You know it when you see it. Or when you *hear* it. And *taste* it. The real Oakland is Festival at the Lake, it's Black Panthers, it's Paramount theater, it's dusty brick, it's scrap metal rusting behind chain-link fences, it's clean Cadillac's riding on vogues, it's a whole lot of people of different colors living on the same block."

Alex nodded. "And he's only a teenager. No wonder we look at newcomers like 'What's your excuse?'"

"Yeah, we passed through . . . mixed-looking neighborhoods on the way over," Tiffany said.

"How you mean 'mixed,' sweetheart? Like a drink?" Charles Lawson, the club's owner, emerged through a side door like a blues note; his smooth stride reverberating with soul. To Alex he extended a hand, brown and warm as the top-shelf brandies with which he was known to stock the bar.

"Sorry to disturb you, old friend," Alex said while offering a smile.

"Watch yourself now, talkin' all that 'old' stuff," Charles replied with a chuckle. "I can keep pace with you young cats, whatever game we playin'. How's it going?"

"Can't complain. And yourself?"

Charles leaned his elbows on the counter. "Things have been slow lately. Catering to a new clientele, if you know what I mean. The youngsters don't want to hear us testifying about hard times. Maybe because to them there ain't none. And then, just the other day, I saw these two suits, couldn't have been much older than you, sweet talkin' my landlord. Them boys had the nerve to say they would let my restaurant live as long as the name changed to something more *universal*. Like 'Jumping Acorn' is too Oakland-centric, y'know? Anyhow, won't you introduce me to this lovely friend of yours?"

"This is Tiffany," said Alex.

The woman smiled. "I'm relatively new to Oakland, and Alex is showing me some sights."

"We got hungry," added Alex, "so I figured she needed a Lawson

Special, best fish fry in town."

"Indeed," said Charles, throwing on an apron. "Have a seat. Tom, bring our guests a couple Half-and-Halfs on the house."

Alex and Tiffany took a table closest the wall so Tiffany could continue perusing the photos while Alex identified a few more of the less-notable faces, among them comedian Mark Curry and singer Goapele. Tom set down a pair of iced tea-and-lemonades served in mason jars. The aromas of onion, garlic, lemon-pepper, and paprika soon filled the air, and Charles's cheerful whistling could faintly be heard above a tempting sizzle.

"You're gonna love this meal, I promise," Alex said after clinking glasses with Tiffany.

"I'm glad you brought me here. Sounds like this place might not exist much longer."

"I'd watch your mouth, in all due respect. Nobody's going to push Charles out. Not as long as he's been here, not with all he's meant to the city."

"Maybe not. But some kind of change is inevitable, right? I mean Charles implied as much."

The food arrived. The crisp, golden, hot sauce-drizzled flavorgasm that was fried catfish *ala* Charles Lawson had been known to resurrect the deadest of appetites (as the many framed reviews attested). While Alex and Tiffany enjoyed their meal, the space fell silent save for Tower of Power's brassy reverberations emanating from wall speakers.

"Is this not the best thing you've eaten?" asked Alex.

"It just might be. If the neighborhood's really in danger of losing this place, it would seem there's a responsibility, among anyone who really cares, to ensure that doesn't happen. Now, how that can actually be done, I'm not sure. But, hey, worth a try."

"There you go," said Alex.

After finishing their food and saying goodbye to Charles and Tom, they strolled down Broadway toward the water; Tiffany seeming contemplative, Alex staying quiet so as not to interfere. Briny tinges of the Bay wafted on the breeze while rumbles of a passing freight train echoed in the distance.

Crossing Fourth Street, they entered the Produce District where the "dusty brick" of Tom's *real* Oakland was personified by warehouses to which semis delivered fruits and vegetables as hungry gulls soared lulling circles overhead.

"Where are we going?" Tiffany finally asked, the slant of her long, graceful neck casting a bird-like shadow across the pavement.

"I figure no tour of Oakland is complete without a stop at Jack London Square. Sure, everyone *thinks* they know it . . . Heinold's and Jack's little log cabin . . . but I've got a couple rare gems in mind."

At the opposite corner, beneath the shade of a grocery store awning, a man in a tweed coat and khaki fedora had set up a table, and attracted a small crowd, as he hyper-speed swapped a trio of face-down playing cards.

"Hey, look," Tiffany said, "I've never seen this in real life, only on that old Run-DMC video."

Alex chuckled. "It's Tricky."

They watched the hustle for several moments, and then Tiffany asked, "What do *you* do? I mean, I don't guess these tours are your only gig."

Alex considered. Although his hustler's intuition had guided him through many schemes, he had vowed to never scam.

"A little of this, a little of that," he said at last.

heroes with gyros

In another circumstance, Pete Saropoulos would have questioned the decision to enter the highly competitive world of mobile cuisine by opening a food truck despite lacking culinary experience beyond a handful of jobs as a line cook. But the man with the plan was his best friend Alex Kouros. Alex deadened skepticism by presenting Pete with a detailed business plan and menu for the entrepreneurial venture to be named "Taste of Olympus," offering classic Greek fare with an American twist: Roast lamb sandwiches featuring a lemon-mint aioli spread; fries seasoned with lemon, feta cheese, and oregano; *saganaki* "bites," and "village-salad wraps." Even *baklava* gelato for dessert. According to Alex, a majority of the food preparation and cooking would be done in his home kitchen. Allured by the formidable plan, Pete blessed the truck with airbrushed script reading 'Mythic Flavors' above his vivid mural of the Ancient Greek gods enjoying a supreme feast. Meanwhile, Alex secured the necessary certification permits, and purchased food.

At their service site in Jack London Square, they catered to customers until well after midnight. Pete found interacting with crowds to be his favorite part of the night. Despite the hectic pace and constant demands, he enjoyed seeing people savor the food Alex had prepared; an aspect of their culture shared with the public at large, so many different nationalities and ethnicities relishing a taste of Greece. After all the planning and preparation that had gone into launching the enterprise, things were running relatively smoothly—until that Friday night two weeks into the adventure. Neither Pete nor Alex, so wrapped up in catering to customers, initially noticed the problem.

"What can I get for you, sweetheart?" Alex had asked as he leaned out the service window to greet yet another bright-eyed, ruby-lipped, twenty-something woman, the likes of which seemed to make up a large portion of their clientele. Pete added another batch of *kefalotiri* cheese cubes to the fryer for the *saganaki* bites, and heard Alex call to him: "*Ela, Panayioti, thos mou ena horiatiki salata . . .*"

Pete jogged to the fridge and fetched one of the village-salad wraps. He almost dropped it when a horn blared a trio of nearby warnings. "What the hell is that about?" Pete asked.

Alex shrugged. "Who cares? Just give me the wrap!"

Pete waited until after Alex had completed the order, and then said, "Those honks were for us. Better come look at this. I'll cover you for a minute." He swapped spaces with Alex, and then glanced over his shoulder in hopes of gauging his friend's reaction to the new food truck beside them. Its flanks were painted blue-and-white, and emblazoned with a warrior's helmet above the name, "HEROES WITH GYROS." A burly man with a slick mane and sleek eye glasses, which caught the moonlight to equip him with a glowing stare, emerged from the truck. He motioned for Alex and Pete to join him on the sidewalk.

"Hey, I think that's Billy Zamboukis from San Leandro," said Alex with a chuckle. "His pops owns Z's Diner, right? I didn't know Billy was in the food truck game, though. Better go see what he wants."

Pete spread his palms. "Why me?"

"Because," said Alex, "you're a lot more friendly under stress."

With a sigh, Pete exited the mobile sanctuary. The night air and street sounds seemed amplified without the womb-like insulation of the truck. The man was indeed Billy Zamboukis, though Pete knew him only in passing. He stepped up and extended his hand. "Long time, Billy, how's it going?"

But Billy just put his fists to his hips. "*Ti kaneis etho? Emeis menoume afto toh dromo, re malaka!*"

Judging by Billy's tone, this didn't appear to be one of those instances that the word "*malaka*," which basically translated to "jerk-off," had been used as a term of endearment. Pete took a breath. "What's the problem?"

"Oh, you want to talk English so all the *Amerikanee* can understand? Fine. We got this area claimed already! What're you doing selling Greek food here, too?"

Pete glanced back to his truck where Alex leaned out the service window to handle yet another order, seemingly oblivious to the drama unfolding just a few feet away, though customers slowly gravitated toward it. "Hey, man," Pete said with spread palms, "we've been at this for a good two, almost three, weeks and we've never seen your truck. We always park here."

"Well, *we* move around," Billy clarified, "but this is our territory. This whole side of town!"

Pete fought temptation to remind Billy that, technically, he wasn't even from Oakland and therefore had no real authority to state such a claim. But he instead said, "This is a big city, brother. I'm sure there's room for two Greek food trucks."

"No way, man. Mexican trucks? Yeah, there's plenty of them, but you don't see more than one Dominican truck, one Creole truck. I had this niche covered long before you. We'll head on down the road tonight, but next week I better not catch you *malakas* here."

"Big man making big threats," Pete said. He rejoined Alex and tried to explain the ordeal, but his friend seemed preoccupied with the late rush. It wasn't until they shut down for the night that Pete conveyed the full extent of their apparent rival's displeasure. Alex, per usual, downplayed the situation, claiming Billy Zamboukis to be a notorious blowhard full of empty talk.

By the time the profitable weekend ended, Pete felt equally at ease about the Billy Zamboukis situation. "Taste of Olympus" had already gained something of a consistent following. But the next Friday evening, as they pulled up to their usual block, Pete's stomach dropped. Beneath the street lamp, an almost sinister glint cast off the ancient warrior's helmet in the mural on Billy's truck.

They met Billy at the curb in front of their respective vehicles, the "hero with gyros" standing with hands in his pockets, lower lip bulging with what figured to be chewing tobacco given the rust-colored stars of saliva spattering the asphalt near his feet.

"*Ela, Vasili,*" Alex said, "How are you, man?"

"Doing okay, Alex," Billy replied before firing another brownish blob of spit into the gutter. "Nice wheels you got there. Never took you for a culinary artist, what brings you into the food truck game?"

"Aw, you know me, brother," said Alex, "always on top of the trends. Truthfully, my mom's the real culinary artist, I just bridge that gap between her and the people. Folks in the Bay travel far and wide to find great Greek food, so why not bring it to 'em, right?"

"See, that's the thing, though," Billy remarked. "Like I already told Pete, you guys weren't supposed to be back here, and I have to figure out what to do now that you are."

"Sorry for intruding on your space, I really am. How about we stay here, just for tonight, and challenge you to a friendly competition? If you bring in more customers, we'll be at a new spot tomorrow. If we bring in more customers, you let us stay. How's that sound?"

Alex's words were laced with honey, but Pete—watching their rival spit more tobacco residue— doubted Billy would swallow the suggestion given his penchant for more brackish flavors. To Pete's surprise, Billy said, "All right, man. I'll bite."

The trio returned to their respective vehicles and awaited the inevitable crowds. When customers arrived, Pete and Alex fell into their usual steady rhythm. Before long, it became evident that people preferred a "Taste of Olympus."

"Well, shit," said Billy Zamboukis. "A deal is a deal, so I guess you outdid me this time."

The following Saturday evening, Alex and Pete drove over to Jack London Square to find that Billy had parked his rig in such a way that blocked access to their usual service site. Alex honked the horn, and there came a roar from Billy's truck as the ignition fired. Rather than make room, however, he drove straight toward them. Alex maneuvered his vehicle out of the path, and then turned around to back into the space, but Billy came at them again.

Alex floored the gas, and they found themselves speeding away from the waterfront and soaring on Broadway toward downtown, Billy's truck in pursuit. As Pete dug his nails into his seat cushion—his view through the windshield a blur of traffic lights—he couldn't help but think that actual car chases were nothing like the movies. The real thing held none of the Hollywood glamour; only try-not-to-shit-yourself terror. They weren't even going that fast, and yet it seemed they were perpetually moments away from a deadly collision. Alex jerked the steering wheel to-and-fro in search of clear paths around traffic. Horns blared, and tires squealed. But Pete and Alex kept right on past the Paramount Theater and along Auto Row. They zoomed by car dealerships featuring sporty vehicles that would have served them far better under the circumstances.

They made quite a sight barreling up the road: a pair of food trucks, decorated with imagery inspired by ancient Greece. A couple waiting at a corner AC Transit stop missed their ride as the bus pulled to the curb, then took off without them while they stood staring open-mouthed at the truck chase. Pete expected to hear sirens at any moment. But a glance in the side mirror revealed no cop cars trailing them, only Billy's truck edging ever closer.

"What the fuck is that malaka trying to pull?" Pete hollered while craning around in his seat to get a better view. "I'm hoping you have a plan here?"

"Sorry," muttered Alex through clenched teeth as he swung the truck down a side street, its tires emanating a bitter, burning scent, "but that's not the case." He took a left, then a right, then another right in hopes of losing Billy. When they found themselves coursing up Broadway again the Zamboukis truck still tailed. Then Alex lost control and sent the vehicle rumbling onto the curb to collide with a fire hydrant. A geyser of water spewed into the sky and across the truck's hood.

"Shit!" said Alex, "You okay? It was an accident!"

Pete's heart thudded in his throat, but he managed to answer in the affirmative. Billy had come to a halt behind them, and was now making angry gestures and shouting out the window, though his rants were mostly inaudible. As Alex breathed deep in an effort to restore his cool, Pete doubted Billy was above murdering them.

Alex was already out of the truck to face Billy who had exited his rig as well. Pete heaved an exasperated sigh and joined his friend on the curb. With his phone he photographed the crash damage.

"What the hell was that?" bellowed Alex.

"You're going to take away all my business!" Billy said, his eyes wild.

"I know we made a deal, but this is my main source of income, not just a *hustle*."

"Nearly getting us all killed is your way of dealing with competition?" Pete asked.

Billy just shrugged his hulking shoulders. "I snapped! I don't tend to do well when stressed."

"There's gotta be a sensible way to compromise," said Alex with a pensive stroke of his chin. "Y'know, Pete and I haven't been at this long and, despite our early success, I've questioned whether this gig is really for me."

"You *have*?" Pete asked.

"The late nights, the bookkeeping, the constant trips to the grocery store," Alex went on, "it's all taking its toll. So, this is my proposition: I'll give you our truck—"

"*What*?" said Pete.

"You can paint over it and add your HEROES WITH GYROS logos, of course—in exchange for part ownership in your operation. Pete and I'll split ten percent of the profits, and we'll give you our recipes. How's that sound? We Greeks have to come together, y'know?"

Although still somewhat stunned by this turn of events, Pete supposed it was a pretty smart ploy. Billy seemed to mull it over a good while before asking, "Are you serious right now?"

"Absolutely," replied Alex. "Look, why don't you sleep on the offer. Meanwhile, Pete and I will lay low for the weekend and enjoy some time off for a change."

"Fair enough," said Billy. "Sorry for spazzing out there. Guess I gotta get back into anger management workshops, after all."

"Apology accepted," Alex said, "you're certainly a passionate guy. Just use that passion for good."

Billy took off his glasses to polish them with the edge of his shirt.

Sans the sleek eyewear, his face adopted a new softness. "Say, you guys go ahead and park wherever you want tonight," Billy remarked.

The next morning, Pete awoke with a call from Alex telling him that Billy had accepted their offer. "And you're *sure* about doing this?" Pete asked.

"I think it's a great deal," said Alex. "We just hustled our previous hustle, and now we're going to get paid for basically doing nothing. That's the ultimate goal, right? Keep climbing until you can rest easy at the top."

"Billy will have two trucks now, so maybe we can run the other one."

"And become *employees* of Mister Zamboukis? No way. We'll help him find a staff, but that's it. We're part owners, remember?"

"Yeah," said Pete, "never mind. I was just thinking aloud. Say, man, I have this feeling you knew about Heroes with Gyros all along, and your plan from the beginning was to get your own truck, gain success, and then flip it for profit." A brief silence on the other line before Pete heard Alex chuckle.

"Maybe," Alex said, "maybe not."

"So, what do you think of the name 'Heroes with Gyros' anyway?"

"It's catchy. Certainly better than the first name I thought up for us."

"Which was?"

"'You'll never guess.'"

At call's end, Pete stared at his lock screen for a long moment before cycling through his recent photos. He paused at the previous night's snapshot of the chase aftermath. The 'Heroes' truck sported a gnarled front bumper. In the camera flash, the vehicle's chrome lip appeared contorted into a sort of smirk; the face of a wounded warrior little worse for wear.

Joy-ride
July

Tank-top temperatures or forego-a-T-shirt-altogether weather. For ladies it meant sports bras and short skirts, sundresses and flip-flops. Too hot to stay inside, even with AC. But outdoors, beneath the sun, people seemed to melt where they stood, reduced to sweaty pulps who spoke of rain as though it were an alien thing. In no way a customarily moderate Oakland summer. By June, local media coined the trend a "heat storm" which made necessary "spare the air" days. Carpooling and public transit were encouraged alternatives to solo commutes. But a decrease in vehicles on the freeways meant more left unattended in parking spaces. By Independence Day focus on the "heat storm" had cooled in favor of new headlines proclaiming the month of "Joy-ride July."

Before he'd even heard the term, Alex Kouros confronted its truth. Like most residents, he had spent a majority of the summer indoors. But upon leaving his home one afternoon, a fresh batch of HEROES WITH GYROS T-shirts slung over his shoulder, the new reality shook his core like a stomp of breaks.

He stood outside his bungalow, contemplating the curbed vehicles, sun glinting off metal-and-chrome in angry bursts like sparks from a welder's torch. He withdrew his car keys, and then remembered his customary spot had already been swiped when he'd returned home from a grocery run hours earlier. He trudged down the block, hoping to spot someone, anyone, out on a stroll, a potential customer on whom he could unload at least one of the new graphic Tees. But, unsurprisingly, no one else appeared, Alex the lone soul foolish enough to venture beyond cool confines at this hour.

Still no sign of the car. He didn't recall leaving his ride this far down 40th Street, but the weather had a way of warping both distance and memory. Up ahead the asphalt shimmered with sparkles of broken glass in the middle of which lay, like a war casualty, the little *evzone* statuette usually dangling from his rearview mirror.

With the tip of his sneaker he nudged at the shards, listened to them crackle. He knelt to pick up the figurine, pocketed it, and then let loose a single *fuck*, the exclamation instantly swallowed by a blistering gust of wind. He went through the usual cycle of shock, denial, and disbelief, perhaps quicker than most. The Chevy had been good to him over the years, racking so many miles along the grind. At least insurance would cover the loss. He took a deep breath and made for BART a few blocks away, determined not to let the misfortune ruin his afternoon.

At the crosswalk adjacent to the train station, a 1980's Cutlass—red save for the primer-colored back door—idled with a frame-rattling bass-boom. The driver cut the stereo as a pit bull-necked passenger leaned through the window and called out, "My man! You interested in a new MacBook Pro? We got one boxed up, fresh from the store."

Alex peered through the tinted rear window where another hulking figure cradled a cardboard package. "No, thanks . . . unless you want to trade for an unlocked iPhone?"

The shotgun passenger made a face and the car burned away.

Alex ascended the steps to Pete Saropoulos's apartment. When his friend opened the door, Alex wondered if, by some nasty coincidence, Pete had also found himself without wheels. He stood with shoulders hunched, and face pale, his customarily close-cropped beard appearing down-right shaggy.

"Someone gank your wheels, too?" Alex asked.

Pete only blinked. "What are you talking about?"

"Looking like that, you must've just had *something* stolen and, come to think of it, I didn't see your car outside."

"Because Joey up the street's letting me keep it in his garage. No way I'd leave my ride by the curb like these other fools 'sparing the air.' Not during 'Joy-ride July.'"

"At least one of us stays informed when it counts," Alex replied with a laugh, following his friend inside.

"Someone took *your* car? Handling it pretty well."

"Yep, still smiling. What's your excuse?"

Alex plopped onto the sofa, setting the shirt stack on its arm. His friend, after a detour into the kitchen from which he returned holding a pair of chilled Heineken bottles, took the adjacent lounge chair. Pete had cracked the windows, citing the modest apartment's overworked AC. Over the rancorous traffic, Alex tried unsuccessfully to catch suspect sounds. He instead tuned his ears to his friend's somber confessions.

"That group show with the gallery downtown?" Pete said. "A total bust, dude. People spaced out in front of my stuff like paintings in a fuckin' doctor's office. I gotta find the right spot for my work, a place that fits me." Indicating the stack of T-shirts, he asked, "What's with those?"

Alex unfolded one. Its front image featured a pita-wrapped sandwich speared atop a sword's tip and back-dropped by the Greek flag draped over the Bay Bridge, above which was printed, in A's colors, HEROES WITH GYROS. "Your drawing makes a great graphic, just like I thought. Gotta figure Billy will want to start selling these out of the truck, maybe give them away with every purchase, at least for a while, as a new promotion. We build a dual-purpose street team to promote the art and food all at once. Win-win for Billy and for us."

"Better remind Billy to leave the truck in a safe spot."

Alex snorted. "Nobody's going to steal a food truck. Come to think of it, Billy was driving hella slow during the car chase. Smooth getaway, not so much."

They sat around watching movies into the sweltering evening, and then, just after dark, a wince-worthy crunching sound off screen. Alex, closest the window, went to investigate. Beneath the dim glow of a sputtering streetlamp, a figure in dark jeans-and-hoodie hunched beside a newish Nissan.

Alex, leaning into the night, hollered through cupped hands, "Swiper, no swiping! Swiper, no swiping!"

Like a skittering roach, the figure retreated, and Alex regarded Pete with a grin. "I'll go ahead and add vigilante to my resume now."

"And the owner of that Nissan will gladly offer himself as a reference, I'm sure. How do you even know that cartoon?"

Alex shrugged. "My little cousin makes me watch it with her. She swears I'll eventually get stumped by Dora's questions. Anyway, that Nissan owner should know better than to drive one of the most boosted cars ever. Unlike our truck, way too inconspicuous."

Pete snapped his fingers. "That gives me an idea."

Alex raised an eyebrow. "That's my line."

Pete's 1974 Beetle more closely resembled a grasshopper with its bulbous insect eyes and sloping hood. Even with run-of-the-mill vanilla paint, the vintage Bug always stood out on the street. After purchasing the ride around his eighteenth birthday, Pete often cruised to-and-from the art store where he loaded up the trunk with hundreds of dollars worth of spray paint, canvas, acrylics, brushes, and the like. This practice left him vulnerable to thieves willing to risk boosting a less common car for such, potentially, high reward. The vehicle had nearly been stolen at least a half dozen times over the last seven years, but apparently prospective thieves hated stickshifts. Still, given its prized cargo, Pete wanted to finally render the car, at least in theory, completely theft proof. In his mind, such a project required not a high tech alarm, but instead only new paint, already in ample supply.

Joey Ruiz was a six-foot-five, three-hundred-thirty pound former high school football player-turned-mechanic and auto detailer whom Pete had met some years ago when he'd been commissioned to create a colorfully plumed Aztec eagle warrior mural on the side of Joey's body shop. Joey so loved the mural that he offered to host Pete's car painting session in addition to letting him use the carport for vehicle storage.

Alex sat on a battered folding chair in Joey's garage while Pete, resembling some Hazmat-protected pandemic survivor, lumbered around in full jumpsuit and mask. Though the well-insulated depot provided relative relief from the triple-digit afternoon, Alex doubted his friend felt very cool in either context. But before Alex could comment, Pete handed him an identical mask.

As Pete wielded the gun, the candy coat sloshed in its tank like toxic ooze and added to the "Hazard Team-leader" vibe of his outfit. In careful, sweeping strokes, over the course of the next hour, he laid the green coat that at last gifted his vehicle with an oh-so-appropriate grasshopper tone. Admiring from a distance, Alex stood with arms crossed over chest, Darth Vader-huffing through the clunky air filter.

Pete removed the detail tape and filled in the resulting lines with gold paint to create laser-like pinstripes along the hood and flanks. Finished, the vehicle's new Oakland A's-inspired metal flake color scheme shimmered beneath the halogens.

Come nightfall, instead of parking in the garage Pete found a space in view of his apartment window. Alex followed him up to his flat. "Look, man. Its past ridiculous now. I know you like keeping the tarp over your creations as long as possible, but what's this all about?"

Pete went to the window. "This is a test-run of my new gig. Everybody's getting these gentrified cars stolen, right?"

"According to the news."

"So, why not offer to paint people's cars, do them up real special, as a way to keep thieves clear? You said it yourself: the food truck's too conspicuous to get boosted. Let's take the same approach with this. You help me get word out, receive a cut of profits, and my art gets a mobile showcase. Everybody's happy."

Alex raised his eyebrows. "Idea's so good, I'm surprised it isn't mine!"

That evening, things remained relatively silent outside Pete's apartment. But the next night squealed and whined with the whir of tires, multiple burnouts left the breeze exhaust-heavy, and the asphalt out front appeared burnt rubber-scarred. The neighborhood, though usually tranquil, seemed like Rip-off Row, echoing with the pastime of car thieves. Prior to two nights earlier, the one on which Alex had prevented a potential theft, Pete's side of town had been spared much illicit activity. Now, however, it seemed a major draw for criminals who had perhaps just discovered a new hot spot.

In Pete's apartment, Alex stood before the window surveying the adjacent curb where the Beetle had again been parked. Beneath a full moon's watery radiance it shone bright as a beacon, an eerie insect green; bug bait meant to lure those possessing fishy motives.

"Under any other circumstance," Pete said, "I'd probably regret moving to Oakland. But right now I'm excited."

Alex chuckled. "Didn't get much of this out in San Ramon, huh?"

"To say the least."

"How long's the 'Dub been sitting out there, three hours or so? I say we're overdue for a few tugs on the line."

From out of the shadows emerged a suspicious shape: a man in a beanie cap and bulky jacket with what appeared to be a crowbar. Alex and Pete held their breath when the stranger neared the Volkswagen. He appeared to do a double-take, nearly bypassing the vehicle before backtracking. The stranger placed a tentative hand on his crowbar. Finally, instead of drawing the tool, he disappeared into the darkness.

With Alex riding shotgun, suggesting ideal routes through the city that would gain his work optimal exposure, Pete cruised the mean green Beetle. They rolled through his neighborhood, and others that had been severely struck by the crime spree, like Fruitvale, and Lakeshore Avenue where they parked in front of the Grand Lake Theater, and The Cheese Steak Shop to entice the movie and lunch crowds. Pedestrians asked to take pictures with the candy Volkswagen, inquiring as to the origins of such a beauty. Once they learned Pete had painted the Bug, they wanted him to do the same for their cars. Alex merely stepped in later to gather customer info and give price-range estimates.

As he took in the scene from the bottom of the driveway, Alex couldn't help chuckle. He didn't want to laugh at someone's distress, especially someone willing to pay for help, but the kid looked ready to sink to his knees in homage while Pete circled the car with the careful mannerisms of a seasoned thief. In the week-and-a-half since he and Pete had begun conducting their ride-arounds in the Beetle, Alex had several times witnessed this display: his friend sizing-up vehicles as they had seen burglars do, the ritual serving both as a way to impress clients with his "knowledge of criminal instinct," and give Pete time to draft a mental sketch of the next makeover. It helped when the vehicle's owner had his or her own vision, but there were days, like today, when that wasn't the case.

"Tell you the truth," the kid began, a wide-eyed beanpole of a nineteen-year-old, "I'd rather let you do what you want." His gaze went down the curb where the VW gleamed green-and-gold amid the scorching afternoon. "You obviously know how to pimp a ride . . ."

Alex, suppressing an all-out laugh, feigned a cough into his fist.

"My favorite color's orange," the kid continued, "just work with that."

Pete offered a quick nod. "2011 Toyota Camry. Number five on this year's list of most stolen cars. Blends in real nice with several other similar compacts. Isn't that right, Alex?"

Alex climbed the driveway, gave his friend a wink. "Relatively quick acceleration, pretty quiet. Your parents buy this for you?"

The kid nodded. "Birthday present."

"That explains it," said Alex.

Pete placed a hand on the kid's shoulder. "I can't promise magic, Kyle, but I can provide something almost as powerful. Normally, my friend and I would take your ride to our garage, but over the phone you mentioned it was okay to work here?"

"Sure."

Alex helped unload the Beetle of supplies. Moving the painting operation outdoors, at least on occasion, had also been his idea, another way to gain free advertising while putting on something of a show; Pete due to command a wider following if people could bear witness to his expertise. Today marked the first outdoor customization session since they'd embarked on this latest entrepreneurial adventure.

By the time he and Pete had taped and primed the vehicle, spectators were gathered curbside, lured as much by the bio-terror-looking respiratory gear as by thunderous bass of The Luniz's "I Got Five On It" bumping from speakers. Alex took off his mask and stepped aside to let the real work commence. He joined the small crowd watching Pete coat the vehicle with a candy tangerine hue that gleamed under the sun.

Once the subsequent orange coats were laid, Pete loaded his gun with a new color and hovered near the Camry again. Whereas his maneuvers in regard to the Beetle had been precise—auto detail tape unraveled to allow for deliberately placed pin stripes—Pete appeared to riff now with the spontaneity of a Jazz musician. Here and there, he added notes of red and gold, his lines melding into one another as though by their own volition.

Finished, Pete stepped back as spectators started asking questions all at once, and Alex heeded the call while fielding phone numbers and job requests. Over his shoulder, he saw Kyle take in the pimped-out ride.

"What do you think?" asked Alex.

"This is just so, hella . . . *dope*!"

Alex smiled. "Spread the word." As the crowd dispersed he remembered his merchandise, and popped the Beetle's trunk to snag one of the HEROES WITH GYROS shirts. "On the house. Looks like a good fit."

Kyle took the Tee and admired the sword-and-sandwich graphic. "Think I've eaten at your truck. This is perfect for my friend."

"What size do they wear?" asked Alex. "We've got a bunch in the back."

"Great. Give me all of 'em."

"Huh? Slow your roll..."

"My buddy just opened a little clothing shop, Cornerz Clothing, over by the lake. He's a local, just like y'all. I'm sure he'd love to carry these, and you guys can work out a consignment deal or something."

Alex fingered his chin. "Let him know we'll be in touch."

"Thanks, guys. And, hey. 'It's all Greek to me,' right?"

Alex bit his lip to stifle a smirk. "Sure thing."

Alex turned to Pete and said, "Job well done. We have new clients lined up, and a possible secondary outlet for the T-shirts. I'd say it was a good day."

Pete chuckled. "All in a day's hustle."

Alex grinned. "Wait 'til our dads see this."

Pete laughed hard before echoing his friend's sentiment.

Local journalists clamored to do a story on Pete the Greek, "Bay Area street artist-turned-custom-auto-painter combating the recent wave of car thefts one mobile masterpiece at a time." No longer was a lack of notoriety an issue for Pete. Meanwhile, Alex managed the money and the operation's overall smooth flow. In short, the hustle was prime. One evening, following yet another auto painting session, Pete turned to Alex: "It's been weeks since you got your insurance money. When are you going to get a new ride?"

Alex contemplated a swarm of gnats hovering in the streetlamp glow like a cloud of metal flake. "I'll go shopping soon as we know this hustle is really making the streets safer."

Pete made a face. "That might take forever to know. I guess getting your ride stolen really spooked you!"

Alex shrugged. "Naw. I just kinda warmed up to catching AC Transit."

By the end of summer, accompanying a much needed relief from the heat, statistics touted a drop in the city's auto thefts. Some said cooler weather had tempered tensions in the streets, joyriders no longer hot to risk a stolen car in chasing an elusive breeze. The media praised an increase in police presence. Those in the know paid their respects to Pete the Greek, performer of aerosol miracles. The painting hustle stayed scorching.

It seemed that for every nine vehicles on the road in Oakland, a tenth was decked out in Willy Wonka hues. The September streets started to look like a Town variation of Hot August Nights, minus the Vegas glitz and muscle cars. Instead, typically bland models—mid-nineties Honda Accords and Civics, Toyota Corollas, Jeep Cherokees—resembled souped-up speedsters, at least in respect to their candy colors. Rush hour literally glowed with metal-flake iridescence. There seemed little doubt that the shimmer of polychromatic paint in vibrant tones of red, green, blue, even occasional purples and pinks, kept thieves at bay.

Fully convinced, Alex, accompanied by Pete, finally visited one of the many dealerships along Broadway Auto Row. Armed with insurance money, Alex gravitated toward a white 2010 Audi A6. The salesman tried to steer him toward a flashier color. Alex plainly stated that the hue didn't matter much since he planned on getting the vehicle custom painted anyhow.

The salesman's eyes narrowed in sudden recognition. "I know you from that article in the *East Bay Express*. You're the guys who paint the cars!"

Alex gestured toward Pete. "Well, he's the painter. I just handle the PR."

"Right on, bro's!" exclaimed the salesman, offering a thumbs up. He flashed a smile. "I manage this lot's social media, and wouldn't mind doing the same for you guys. I'd even strike you a deal..."

Alex slipped the salesman a business card.

Their popularity around town boosted business at the food truck. Within a matter of weeks Billy Zamboukis saw sales increase one-hundred fold.

One afternoon Alex drove his ride, now boasting a "Chameleon" paint job, along Adeline to CORNERZ CLOTHING carrying the exclusive HEROES WITH GYROS shirts. Unassuming from outside, the storefront shop's interior boasted photo collage wallpaper composed of Oakland street signs. Upon entry, the proprietor, a stout, gold grilled Filipino guy named DJ greeted Alex.

"Just the man I been wantin' to see. You hit me with, what, fifteen shirts to start? Bro, we down to our last two! I gotta say, in the past twelve, fourteen days, they been flyin' off the rack!"

Pocketing his funds, Alex said, "Thanks, buddy. I'll get you more soon."

"Good, good. I been seein' Pete's work everywhere lately, bro! He's probably jammed with projects, but I got a buddy George who wants his car done if Pete can make time."

"Shouldn't be a problem."

"Nice. I'll pass on Pete's card. We born-and-bred Oaklanders gotta stick together."

Alex, first to arrive at the garage, found a parking space out front. The warm Autumn morning promised a blistering afternoon as clouds broke toward the horizon. He wondered if the weather change came as an omen. The heat would halt a recent trend of seasonally average temps, and who knew how people would respond.

The insect-green Beetle pulled up a few minutes later, and Pete greeted Alex with a fist bump. Inside the garage, as he stepped into his gear, Pete's face beamed with a joy that begged to be spoken.

"Come out with it already, *re*," said Alex. "Can't just be the sunshine that's got you in a good mood."

Pete, zipping his jumpsuit, yanking on his gloves, said, "On the drive over I stopped for gas and ran into Countess Versailles."

Alex raised an eyebrow. "*Nobody's* name is 'Countess Versailles.'"

"She's the lady who runs the downtown gallery where I was part of that group show a while back."

"I remember now. Well, if anyone has a name like Countess Versailles, it's gotta be her."

"Anyway, she said people have been asking about my portfolio, wondering if Pete Saropoulos is Pete the Greek, Pete the Painter. Now she wants to do a solo show of my auto work. Photos, I guess."

"See? A change of perspective, and your hustle paid off. Congrats, man."

George rolled his F-150 into the garage right on schedule. After taping and priming the vehicle, Pete went out to the Beetle to get supplies. He returned empty-handed, however, his expression akin to that of a heat-stroke victim: face pale, parched mouth parted like a screen door.

"What's wrong with you?" Alex asked, handing his friend a paper cone of water from the nearby cooler.

Pete took a sip and color returned to his cheeks. "You'd better come take a look."

The afternoon exhaled a Bay-tinged breeze as Alex stepped out into natural light. Momentarily blinded by the asterisks of sun punctuating vehicle hoods and doors, Alex shaded his eyes. Tragedy fell into focus.

Among the cars lining the curb, Alex and Pete's were the lone models boasting extravagant paint; candy-coated bookends that had been targeted despite their proximity to more traditionally vulnerable models.

"Fuck!" said Alex.

"Maybe these thieves were colorblind?" Pete remarked.

"I think we were the ones with blinders on." While shaking his head in disbelief, Alex couldn't help chuckle. He felt that familiar crunch of glass underfoot as he stepped to the sidewalk's edge. The Audi's passenger window was busted, and frayed wires spilled like exposed veins where Alex's stereo had once been. Figuring his car immune to theft, he never bothered to set an alarm. Meanwhile, Pete's trunk had been lock-picked and left open to reveal a now barren interior.

The two friends stood silent beside their respective rides, assessing the damage, their heads bowed, as though humbled by the scene. When they again converged in the middle of the street, Alex was first to speak, regarding his friend with a slight smile. "Well, they got us, huh?"

Pete gestured toward the Beetle as though it pained him to lift his arm. "To say the least. Shit, I had a couple hundred dollars worth of paint in there. Remember what Ms. Mavromatis said about haters? Like that guy at the food truck. They move in groups, and the evil eye doesn't blink for anyone."

Alex shook his head. "I think there's a story about a king in Ancient Greece who spent all his time fortifying his city, building great Cyclopean walls with huge stone, stationing soldiers up on high lookout points, and training all the young men so they would grow to keep the kingdom safe from barbarians. Come to find out, after so much planning and work, he forgot to pull up the drawbridge."

Pete chuckled. "Maybe I'm biased, but I figure our ancestors were smarter than that."

"Still smarter than us, looks like."

Alex contemplated the horizon where heat waves shimmered like restless ghosts.

Pete picked up a shard of glass, contemplated the play of light, and then chucked it into the gutter. "Now what?"

AUTUMN
ΦΘΙΝΟΠΩΡΟ
2013

Mati

Alex huddled in bed amid the blackness, listening to footsteps shuffle down the hall like those of some old, heavy-footed lioness. As they neared, he pulled the covers closer to his chin in hopes that the grand feline would shamble right by his half-open door. But then a shadow moved across the faint glow emanating from the passage.

His *yiayia*, by that time a week or so into her visit from Greece, tottered across the carpet without so much as a purr. Hunched over, with stealthy steps, she approached his bed. Alex feigned sleep, but kept his eyes slitted to see Yiayia standing directly over him, the mothy scent of her pajamas only slightly dulled by the trace of mint candy on her breath. Alex partially prepared for what would come next. He'd endured these encounters the past seven nights, but they still took him somewhat by surprise.

The woman leaned in close and spit on his forehead. Just the subtlest mist of saliva, but Alex felt himself go rigid with a combination of horror and disgust. Still, he couldn't move for fear his grandmother would discover him awake. So he stayed frozen while the woman continued her ritual; spitting, then crossing herself the way Alex and his family did at church. Most unsettling, however, was the mantra she murmured in between her bouts of subtle expectoration.

"*Tsou, tsou, tsou, exoh matia . . . Tsou, tsou, tsou, exoh matia . . .*"

Alex recognized the Greek, but couldn't decipher its meaning.

The next morning, Alex made a point of rising prior to his grandmother so he could address the "night visits" solely with his parents.

As he sat at the kitchen table spooning Cheerios, he glanced first at his father reading the newspaper, then over at his mother frying eggs atop the stove. Finally he took a breath and said, "Yiayia spits on me at night." There it was. Just in case circumstances called for a quick get-away, from the edge of his chair he tried unsuccessfully to skim the floor with his socked feet.

His father regarded him over the rim of his coffee cup, while his mother turned from the skillet. Finally, Dad chuckled and said, "Don't you understand? Yiayia does that to protect you!"

Regarding his father skeptically, Alex asked, "Protect me from what?"

"The evil eye," said Alex's mother, joining them at the table with two plates of eggs, one for her husband, and the other for Alex. "That's what she protects you from."

"With her *spit?*"

"*Pou einai toh mialo sou?*" Without waiting for a reply, Dad explained, in Greek, "When someone says something nice about you, over and over again, or they cast their gaze on you, whether out of admiration or jealousy, they leave you open to evil spirits. That's why we say, when a person isn't feeling well, or has endured some hardship, 'They must have been struck by the Evil Eye!'"

The Evil Eye.

Alex shuddered, even while uncertain of the phrase's meaning. How could an eye be evil? Staring at the pair of sunny-side eggs that seemed to gaze back at him, he pictured a giant eye cloaked in a dark cape and wielding a sword. "But, how does Yiayia's spit protect me?"

"If someone has given you the Evil Eye," Mom began, "being spit upon will make you seem less precious than you are. If someone's compliments have raised you up too high, Yiayia knocks you back down so the evil spirits won't think you're worth bothering."

"Oh," said Alex. Then after an instant of consideration, he added, "Cool!"

Mom and Dad laughed.

That night, Alex readied for Yiayia's next visit. When the woman came to him in the dark, leaned in and spit on his forehead, he opened his eyes and smiled before exclaiming, "Thanks, Yiayia!"

His grandmother yelped in surprise, and nearly stumbled backward, but gathered herself just in time to join Alex in his laughter. From her robe pocket, she withdrew a silver necklace with a porcelain charm shaped like a blue eye. "Keep this on, and the evil spirits will always stay clear."

While he thrashed beneath his blankets, twenty-five-year-old Alex couldn't summon dreams. Only those childhood memories surfaced behind his eyelids. Finally, he sat up in the early morning darkness, pawing at his neck for the eye charm. He remembered it was at a jeweler's for repair. He would have to leave for work without protection.

In the trees, flashes of rust-color among the green. The air seemed electric with the initial hints of Autumn. The day's first customers—their casual garments spattered with kaleidoscopic patterns of acrylic paint— were participants in Mosswood Park's Saturday afternoon craft fest. In urgently greeting the patrons, Alex Kouros should have figured the restlessness a byproduct of his reduced workload. The reins had been handed over to Billy Zamboukis, afterall. Alex only lended the occasional hand with prep. While pacing the steel confines of the food truck between the salad bar bins of sliced tomatoes, cucumbers, and red onions, he would have been better off shunning the impulse to leave the vehicle to mingle with the crowd.

"I'm guessing this is your gig here?"

Alex looked up. A middle-aged man, dressed in a leather jacket despite the heat, had somehow materialized in the truck. But, as if to establish himself a non-threat, he held out his hand. Alex took it and said, "I'm part owner, and I don't work in the truck much anymore. But today, with the festival, I . . ." He let his voice trail off upon truly meeting the man's gaze. There was something vaguely off-putting about the stranger's eyes: blue like bleach. Alex couldn't look away, despite his unease.

"What's your name, young man?"

"Alex Kouros."

"Ah, so you are Greek. I guessed that by looking at you, but now there's no doubt."

Alex nodded. "Good to meet you, mister . . ."

"Odezmir."

Alex tilted his head to the side. "Turkish?"

Mr. Odezmir smiled. "Indeed. But we can be friends, no? Your lamb sandwiches are the best! The meat is seasoned perfectly! And that lemon-rosemary aioli? Superb! And your magnificent gyros!"

Alex reached for his necklace, again finding it absent. He went woozy with panic. "Mr. Odezmir, time to go. I need to . . . reup for ingredients. You aren't the only fan of our food." As he ducked past Odezmir, Alex shivered, hot and then cold, as though coming down with the flu in the face of all this flattery.

"You don't look so good. What's up?" Alex's friend Pete said when they met up at a coffee shop that evening.

Alex slumped in his chair and tried to stifle a yawn. "I'm pretty sure I have the Evil Eye."

Pete fingered the black scruff on his chin. "Someone gave you the *mati*?"

Alex yawned again. "Think it was this Turkish guy at the food truck."

"Turkish?" Pete said. "Go figure."

"I was feeling sick earlier, now I can't stop yawning. Even more suspicious, while running errands on the way over here, I made sure to feed the meter and still got a damned parking ticket."

Pete nodded. "Actually, I'm not too surprised. It figures someone would eventually get jealous of our food truck grind, especially after the sweet profit deal with Billy. So, what are you going to do?"

Alex rested his elbow on the tabletop, and his chin in his hand. "Too bad both my *yiayias* have passed away. I'm pretty sure the combined power of their saliva would cure me."

"Yeah, nothing like germs to ward off an ailment."

Alex chuckled. "Spiritual ailments have different vulnerabilities than physical ones."

"So, no seeing a doctor then. How about the priest?"

"Nah," Alex said. "This calls for more than a priest, more than a doctor. Maybe a witchdoctor?"

Pete clapped his hands. "What about Ms. Mavromatis? She could help!"

Alex frowned. "No one knows if she's still alive. Or even if she exists."

Pete made a face. "Of course she exists. She was good friends with your *yiayia*. You separate yourself from the Greek community, and no one believes you exist anymore."

"Well, I thought she was just a numbers lady. What can she do for me?"

"She is a numbers lady, and something of a priestess. A keeper of old *horyo* magic . . . if there is such a thing."

"Man," said Alex, "these Amerikani really have you brainwashed."

Pete just laughed. "Anyway, I heard she still lives over by the old church in West Oakland. Can't be that hard to find her. How many Greeks have homes on that side of town these days?"

"So, you game for a funky expedition?"

Pete sighed. "Might not be the best idea, but I did bring her up. Plus, who else is going to watch your back, homie?"

Two days later, on a clear Saturday afternoon, Alex and Pete rode the BART train to West Oakland. Ramshackle Victorian homes with scabby, paint-peeled facades lined the buckled sidewalks like over-sized doll houses belonging to neglected children. Beyond them, on the horizon, the San Francisco skyline—all sharp-angled skyscrapers and big town glitz—rose like the city of Oz.

Alex again examined the paper scrawled with Ms. Mavromatis's address and phone number. Obtaining it had been as easy as leafing through one of Yiayia's old notebooks. Alex and Pete trudged along Seventh Street while pitbulls snarled and frothed from behind fences. Chain link rattled as if to further discourage potential trespassers. The friends advanced with their heads low, but Alex allowed himself a periodic glance beyond the trash-strewn pavement. A scraper zoomed past with the stereo's bass cranked high enough to rattle windows. Alex felt the driver's stare.

As the duo neared Ninth Street, they came upon a house with paint so faded it lent the appearance of old newsprint. Out front stood a black boy and girl; fourteen or fifteen years old at the most. Alex started to stroll on past, but the young man's voice halted him.

"Hey, you know what time it is?"

Alex almost went for his phone, but then remembered he wore a watch today. "It's quarter to two."

The teen only nodded. But when Alex and Pete started on their way again, they heard him call.

"You guys lost?"

Alex asked, "You happen to know where a Ms. Mavromatis lives?"

The teen raised his eyebrows. "Y'all newbies know her?"

Alex made a face. "Bro, we're *from* the Town!"

The teen smiled. "Ah, ok then! She's just over on Castro. But watch yourself, blood. Word is, her new neighbors—young couple from Iowa—kept blasting their music at night. They talked shit to her after she asked them to turn down the beats. So, next day she walked by and shot them a long glance. Soon they didn't feel so good. Longer they stayed home, sicker they got until they finally bailed for real. Turns out they had black mold all up in their house."

Alex raised his eyebrows. "Damn, like *that*?"

"Like that, blood. Be safe out here."

"So, she gave her neighbors the *mati*," Pete said after he and Alex had moved on. "Not only can she cure the Evil Eye, but she can dish it out, too."

"Yup. Now let's hurry before my bad luck catches up to us and we come across someone wanting more than just the time."

Between another scowl of a house and a huge vacant lot of golden weeds, stood the former house of worship for Oakland's Greek Orthodox Christians. Though Baptists now used the church, its domed Byzantine architecture remained intact, down to the Ionian-style pillars. The duo stopped in front to pay respect. Alex even made a sign of the Cross. "Your folks ever attend services here?" Pete asked.

"Nah," said Alex. "By the time our parents immigrated from Greece before we were born, the community already used the church up on Lincoln Ave."

"I wonder about this neighborhood back in the '20s and '30s. The closest we ever got to having a real Greektown, huh?"

"Seems that way."

"Why do you suppose Ms. Mavromatis stuck around?"

Alex shrugged. "Maybe she's better able to practice her spells in relative isolation."

Ms. Mavromatis lived one block up from the church in a brown Victorian taller than it was wide, with white-and-red trim like candy cane piping. Alex and Pete marched up the steps with hungry enthusiasm, though their confidence waned as their initial knocks went unanswered.

"Sure this is the right place?" asked Pete, glancing at the darkening sky as if imagining how it would be to wander this section of town after nightfall.

At last the door opened, but no one was visible; the duo greeted only by the black licorice-scent of anise seed, and the earthy, spicy aroma of clove. Pete and Alex exchanged puzzled glances. Then a good witch of a woman appeared, complete with a gentle smile and flowing ivory dress. She said nothing, only gazed at her visitors for a long moment as though trying to leave an imprint on their foreheads.

"You're Alex and you're Pete," the woman said finally, as if bestowing them with their names. "Welcome."

"Nice to meet you, Ms. Mavromatis," Alex and Pete replied in unison.

"Please. It's Tina." She ushered them inside. The home's interior exuded a warmth which, like the steam emanating from a cup of chamomile tea, soothed the tension in Alex's belly and cleared his head. He and Pete took chairs at the dining room table.

Tina Mavromatis set down a plate of *koulourakia* atop a doily like those found in most Greek homes. She disappeared back into the kitchen, and the tightness in Alex's stomach returned as he listened to her fussing at the sink.

Tina returned with a glass of water, a spoon, and a small bottle of olive oil that she placed in front of Alex before taking a seat across from him. "Your *yiayia*," the woman began as she scooted her chair closer to the table, "was a wonderful woman. Kind and genuine with a deep pride in her heritage and a love for her home country. But above all, she loved her family, and had a special love for you. I got to know her well during the months she spent in the States, and we regularly exchanged letters when she returned to Greece. Up until the day she died, in fact. She spoke of you often and hoped you would grow to be successful and safe."

"How come she never introduced us?" Alex asked.

Tina smiled. "She knew you would seek me out at the right time, and didn't want to get in the way before that time had come. You encountered a stranger some days ago. A man of blue eyes and swarthy complexion."

Alex tried to swallow, but the spit only caught in his throat.

"This man," Tina went on, "of great Turkish lineage, has been watching you for some time, envying the success you've gained through your creative endeavor. He has paid you many compliments, but secretly wishes you harm. And that's why you've come to me. That's why your grandmother knew you'd come."

"Who is he?"

"I cannot tell you. It wouldn't be wise. Just know he is a secret disparager. Remain wary of him."

Glancing at Alex, Pete asked, "So, he actually has the *mati*?"

"I suspect that to be the case," said Ms. Mavromatis. "But there is only one way to be certain."

The woman poured a spoonful of olive oil, and then let two drops fall into the water. Instead of floating, the golden blobs sank and converged at the bottom of the glass. Alex didn't know what that meant, but assumed the worst. Ms. Mavromatis confirmed his fear upon regarding the glass with pursed lips and furrowed brow.

"The *mati* indeed," she said. "Now, we have to rid you of it."

Alex winced. "Will it hurt?"

Ms. Mavromatis didn't answer, but the calmness in her gaze somewhat eased Alex's fears.

To the left of the table, atop a fireplace's mantle, stood five ceramic owl figurines of varying sizes and materials from porcelain to glass; their crystalline eyes shimmering amber in the sunlight beaming through a window. Alex studied them until Ms. Mavromatis came around to his chair. She dabbed olive oil onto his forehead, chin and cheeks in the sign of the Cross before repeating the process on his palms.

Although Ms. Mavromatis bent close to him, her breath smelling of cinnamon, the trio of prayers she uttered in Greek passed too quickly and quietly for Alex to understand. He did vaguely recognize their sound, like a familiar lullaby, as the same tangled utterances Yiayia had used in protecting him that night long ago. Before repeating the process, Ms. Mavromatis spit lightly onto the crown of his head. At ritual's end, Ms.

Mavromatis returned to her chair and plucked another cookie from the tray of *koulourakia*, her previously stern look of concentration giving way to tranquility.

When Alex was about to ask if the spell had been broken, she only put a finger to her lips before gently pushing the plate of sweets toward her guests.

Alex looked over at Pete, who shrugged before biting into his cookie. Alex set his down on the doily, careful to sweep the crumbs into his hand.

"How do you feel?" Ms. Mavromatis asked.

"Not much different. Is the curse gone?"

"Well," said Ms. Mavromatis, "we'll see after your nap."

Alex's eyelids drooped, and then, before he could ask Ms. Mavromatis to clarify, he was sleeping deeply. Upon waking—minutes or hours later?—he felt more rested than he had in several days, free of the vague sensation that he was sinking beneath the gaze of some sinister force. No longer under the *mati's* power, he looked around the room to find that colors appeared brighter, shapes sharper. When he closed his eyes, for just a moment, he saw Yiayia smiling in the darkness. When he opened his eyes again, Pete was staring open-mouthed as if regarding a risen corpse. Ms. Mavromatis, meanwhile, regarded Alex with an expression mirroring Yiayia's loving grin.

shades
of
Other

Friday afternoon during art class, seven-year-old Alex Kouros gained an unexpected response from the teacher after requesting a peach-colored sheet of construction paper during the self-portrait activity.

"For what, Alex?"

From beneath a head of dark curls, loopy and full like those a child might render in a crayon drawing of a boy, Alex gazed up at the tall, blonde woman and said, "To make my face."

Ms. Henderson considered the squares of multi-colored paper fanned in her grasp like a poker hand. "Alex, your skin is more *olive*. Why don't you use this?" Alex recognized Ms. Henderson's tone. It was the same used by his mother when she asked, Why don't you set the dinner table? An order, not a question. He took the vaguely tan paper without further word, comparing it to the pinkish sheets used by Toby Fields and Dave Wilson seated on either side of him.

"Hey, Toby," Alex said, "why'd you keep saying you're just from America when Ms. Reese asked us to name our cultures for the Heritage Flag project?"

Toby shrugged. "I'm just American."

Dave giggled. "Nobody's *just* American. Everybody's from somewhere else. Even if it was a long time ago."

Alex laughed, too. He'd always thought Toby's head looked a little like a pinecone: slight point at the top, yellowish hair jutting out in spiky strands. "Yeah," Alex said, "My parents are from Greece. That means I'm *Greek*-American. Not just American-American."

"Greek like the Spartan warriors in your dad's book?" asked Dave.

Alex nodded.

"If my family was ever from somewhere else," Toby began, "like a really long time ago, it was from somewhere else in America. Maybe not California, okay? Somewhere else."

"Okay, Toby," remarked Dave, "whatever."

Alex got back to his portrait. He felt good about his progress, but still thought the face would look cooler on a lighter shade of paper. He seemed to be the only kid, besides the Asian, Latino, and black ones, with a darkish color. That meant something, though he wasn't sure what.

During the car ride home, Alex studied his project, the Greek flag cut from a coloring page courtesy of Ms. Reese. In the top left corner, a white cross on a blue background, and then stripes alternating blue and white. On a footnote below the flag, Alex had jotted, *The Greek flag has nine stripes for the nine letters in the Greek word for 'Freedom.'* He'd written the word using the Greek alphabet, but had forgotten how to pronounce it.

"Dad, how do you say 'freedom' in Greek again?"

Alex saw his father's eyes like knife blades in the rearview mirror.

"How many times I have to tell you this? The word is *eleftheria*. E-LEF-TH-E-RIA. Okay, you say it."

"*Eleftheria*," said Alex. Now his father's eyes seemed smiley. Alex knew what would make him even happier. "*Paterah*," Alex continued, "*boroumeh na fameh se ena estiatorio apopseh?*" Just as Alex had hoped, in the mirror his father now smiled with his entire face.

"*Bravo sou, re!* That's why we have been send you to Greek School after regular school, your mother and I."

"So, can we, Dad?"

"I'm afraid not, Alex. Money goes to bills, so no restaurant dinner tonight. But I have something even better for us! This evening we have been invited to the home of Mister Saropoulos. Yianni, who has the shop where we get the *spanakopita*. The one the *Amerikani* call 'John the Greek.'"

This brought to mind those visits to Mr. Saropoulos's deli, all the times Alex had pressed his face against the counter window showing bricks of feta cheese. He and his father always savored a chewy bite of grilled octopus before taking home the spinach-and-cheese pie.

"Yianni has a son named Pete who is around your same age."

Alex rubbed his fingertip against the sharp corner of his paper flag. "How come I never met him at church or Greek School?"

"Because Yianni and his family live in San Ramon and go to the church in Concord."

Alex hadn't known of another Greek church in the area aside from the one in Oakland, but it wasn't something he'd given much thought.

En-route to San Ramon, Alex gazed out the backseat window. "My friend Toby is British-American, and my friend Jan is Polish-American. Poland and Britain are in Europe, and so is Greece, right?"

"Well, some also consider Greece to be part of the Far East," Alex's mother clarified. "But, yes, it's in southern Europe."

"So why is our skin so much darker than theirs?" Alex asked. He watched his parents exchange glances.

"Countries like Greece and Italy and Spain are *Mediterranean* countries," his mother said. "Mediterraneans are more tan than those in northern countries because . . . well . . . all the sun, I guess."

Alex considered. "Are there any blonde Greeks? All the people we know from church have brown or black hair like us."

"What about Mister Kondikas?"

"Oh, yeah. So, I guess there are a few."

"Mostly they come from the northern part of the country," Alex's mother said.

"Did you ever wish you had blonde hair and blue eyes?" asked Alex.

"What kind of question is this?" his father snapped. "Why would it be better to have blue eyes?"

"Maybe not *better*," Alex remarked, "but . . . I don't know, never mind."

Against the twilight, Alex's eyes widened as his father led the way into the garden through a gate alongside the house. In their backyard, the Saropoulos family had a swimming pool. The pool was shaped like a giant jelly bean. Alex wanted a pool, but Dad claimed Oakland never got hot enough. San Ramon reminded Alex of summer trips to Greece. Even though the day had ended, the heat remained like a bully sapping his strength until he plopped into one of the plastic chairs arranged among the grass. Mr. Saropoulos stood behind the barbecue, wearing an apron and dodging the smoke billowing up from the grilling meat.

"*Kalo ston Alexandre!*" said Mr. Saropoulos, momentarily abandoning the grill. Alex shook the big man's hand, and then stepped aside to let his father say hello. After greeting Alex's parents, Mr. Saropoulos called over his shoulder, "*Panayioti! Pou eisai? Ela tho tohra!*"

A few moments later, a boy came bounding out of the house, shirtless in the dusk. He stood maybe a head taller than Alex.

"Pete," Mr. Saropoulos said, "say hello to Alex."

"Hi, Alex," said Pete.

"Hey," Alex replied. He followed Pete to another corner of the yard.

"How old are you?"

"Seven-and-a-half," Alex said.

"I'm eight already," said Pete. "Do you like to play video games?"

"Sometimes."

"What do you like to do most?"

"I like to read."

"But what do you like to play? Do you do any sports?"

Alex shrugged. "I play foursquare and kickball with friends at school."

"Do you like doing karate?" Pete mimed a quick punch-and-kick combination, his fist and foot slicing the air just inches from Alex's face.

"Yeah," said Alex, "that's fun."

Pete flashed his gap-toothed grin again. "Let's box! I don't have gloves, but we can use water wings."

A slight tremor rippled through Alex's belly. "Okay."

"We can hit each other," said Pete, "but just soft."

Orange and blue inflated water-wings encircling their fists, the boys traded jabs while bobbing about the middle of the yard. Alex felt plastic brush his chin before countering with a swipe of his own. Out of the corner of his eye he saw his father and Mr. Saropoulos watching while cradling beer bottles, the twilight reflecting off the green glass with an alien glow.

"They are starting to hit harder," Alex heard his father say.

"Because they know we are looking." Mr. Saropoulos replied.

As he again glanced over at his father, Alex got nailed in the stomach. The impact sent him to his knees. His mother and Ms. Saropoulos hurried over.

"Shake it off," said Alex's father.

"Sorry," Alex heard Pete saying, "I'm *really* sorry! It was an accident!"

Later, they ate dinner beneath a dark sky. The moon and a lantern provided the only light as mosquitoes buzzed overhead. The boys sat next to each other. They devoured their meal between gulps of soda while listening to the adults reminisce about money and marriage. But Alex perked up when hearing them recount similar stories of childhoods spent in villages an entire ocean away.

"That donkey was never very nice to me," said Alex's dad, "he had a nasty bite, but oh, did my father love him. Sometimes I think he favored the donkey over us, his own children. The only thing he loved more than the donkey was his wine." The adults erupted in laughter, though Alex wasn't sure why. Mr. Saropoulos filled the wine glass belonging to Alex's father. The men exchanged a nod while toasting beverages.

"Ah," exclaimed Mr. Saropoulos, a cigarette dangling from his lips, "those were the days. Difficult for us to leave Greece and come to America."

"You're telling me," said Alex's father. "But at least we have made some real money here."

There was that word again, Alex thought. Money was important.

Maria Saropoulos, Pete's mother, crossed her arms over her chest and gave her husband a sideways glance. "Money that we give mostly to the government," she said. "I'm about ready to pack up and head *back*."

"Maria, go if it makes you so happy! But the boy stays with me!"

"Ha! The boy *goes* if I go."

The table went quiet as Mr. and Ms. Saropoulos stared each other down. Alex glanced over at Pete who only shrugged. Finally, Alex's father broke the silence.

"Easy now, easy. Let's have more wine."

The adults lifted their glasses, while Alex and Pete went for simultaneous sips of soda.

"I remember, as a small boy," Alex's father began, "sitting in Papa's lap at a *taverna* table while he drank with his friends. All the sudden, he went very quiet and looked off to the distance. Finally, one of his buddies said, 'What is it, Mitso? Why do you appear so sad?' And my father raised his wine glass and replied, 'One day I'm going to die and there'll be no more of this damn stuff for me!'"

More laughter from the grownups, while Alex and Pete exchanged puzzled glances.

After dinner, as the adults chatted over coffee, the boys retreated to Pete's bedroom. From under his mattress he withdrew a magazine with a naked woman on the cover. He flipped it open to a photo spread of two women lying on top of each other. Both had blonde hair like Ms. Henderson, the art teacher.

"Why are they doing that?" asked Alex.

"Because they're lesbians," Pete clarified. "Lesbians are girls who like to kiss each other."

Alex took a breath. "Where'd you get that?"

"I found it in my dad's room," Pete said before returning the magazine to its hiding place. "My mom never goes in there."

"Your parents sleep in different rooms?"

"Don't yours?"

Alex shrugged. "Do you think your mom really wants to go back to Greece?"

Pete mirrored Alex's gesture. "She says that all the time, but I know she'd never actually move away. It's just how her and my dad talk. So, do you have lots of Greek friends, like from your church and stuff?"

"Yeah, but I mostly hang out with my American friends from school. They always want me to teach them bad words in Greek."

"Hopefully, I can come to your house next time," said Pete.

"That would be awesome. Except we don't have a swimming pool."

Pete just shrugged again.

Pictures decorated the bedroom walls, drawings Alex guessed Pete had done; sketches of superheroes and racing cars, even a few wild animals. He spotted a crayon portrait of a shield-and-sword-wielding Spartan warrior in full armor, save for the helmet cradled in his left arm. The warrior's face looked a lot like Pete's. The drawing was better than anything in Alex's coloring book. Alex wished he could draw half as well.

"Yeah, it's supposed to be me," Pete said, apparently following Alex's gaze. "Pretty good, huh?"

"It's great," Alex replied, "except . . . I might have drawn it on a darker piece of paper to get your skin color just right."

"I never thought of that, but it's a good idea. Besides, my Dad always says, 'We're *Greek*, not *white*.'"

Alex smiled. "Hey, did you know the nine blue and white stripes in the Greek flag represent the nine letters in the Greek word for freedom?"

"Duh, my parents told me about a hundred times already. Anyway, you ready to play some video games?"

"Sure," said Alex. "Bring 'em on.

Invisible Friends

Pete Saropoulos arrived at Monte Vista High on a warm spring day, wearing a baseball cap as he sauntered tardy into first-period Freshman English, capturing his classmates' attention when Mr. Jones began to read aloud the opening stanza of Homer's *The Iliad*. Come any reference to Greece, students regarded Pete as an ultimate authority. At the beginning of the year—*freshman* year—new friends in this new district began calling him "The Greek." Pete had grown up here in suburban San Ramon, but it was still as though his otherness needed clarification amid the largely unfamiliar Anglo student-body at his new high school. The nickname caught on, and he wondered, while en-route to his desk on that May morning, if his peers thought "The Greek" might recite the epic from memory right along with the teacher. As if all Greek-Americans, young or old, were born knowing by heart the stories of their ancestors.

The students, however, weren't so much focused on *him* as on his cap. He hardly ever wore hats, but on that particular day he donned one to conceal what lay beneath. Ironically, it seemed the hat itself had brought him unwanted scrutiny. Pete tried to convince himself this was due to his choice of an Atlanta Braves cap, in honor of D'Andre Bryant's birthplace, rather than a San Francisco Giants or Oakland A's.

"Why are you wearing that, man?" one kid asked as Pete sauntered by. He didn't answer, but instead settled into his desk and pulled the cap lower on his head.

At the break period, out on the schoolyard Pete, still sporting his ball cap, received a greeting from his friend D'Andre Bryant, the teen's head cloaked in a grey hoodie. D'Andre pulled it down.

"*Damn!* You cut your dreads off!"

D'Andre shrugged. "I finally got tired of them shits. Plus, I didn't want you to be the only one gettin' funny looks."

"Thanks! Owe you one." Pete at last took off his hat to uncover the cornrow braids running in zig-zag patterns from the top of his forehead to the base of his skull, their ends fastened with tiny rubber bands. "You think *I'll* be getting funny looks?"

"Don't get me wrong, man, my sis hooked you up real nice, except we know these ain't the most open-minded folks. Not sure how you turned out an exception, being from the neighborhood and all."

"Yeah, this is home, but I never really hung out with these kids, and we're the only Greeks on the block. Most of my friends from back in the day are other Greeks who go to the Orthodox church in Oakland."

"Well, I'm glad to be your token black friend in that case."

Pete laughed. "Yeah, right. Why do your folks bus you all the way out to Monte Vista High from Richmond in the first place?"

D'Andre pulled his hood back up. "Mom wants to expand my horizons, whatever that means. See you at lunch."

"See ya," Pete started away, but heard his friend call.

"Wait up. You just gonna stroll in there, no hat or nothin'?"

"I already tried the hat, first period."

"Better hope they don't take your head off."

Upon reaching History class, he wondered if D'Andre had a point. Hand on the doorknob, Pete took a deep breath and remembered why he had coveted the hairstyle to begin with. It looked cool, and he liked it. To hell with anyone else.

No laughter, no whispers. Initially it seemed as though everyone, the teacher included, had leaned forward to place this stranger. Then came the delayed round of gasps as Pete had been recognized. In grand emphasis, Todd Mahoney—a thick-necked O-lineman—let forth an "Oh, shit!" that finally triggered the guffaws.

At his desk Pete felt oddly content until, from behind, he heard mutters and hisses of, "Wanna-be!" He whipped around with a glare, but no one met his gaze. He faced the front of the room again and, though he felt eyes bearing down, tried unsuccessfully to concentrate on Mr. Lawrence's lecture.

"All right, people. All right, now," the teacher said, gesturing for silence. "Let's just settle down. It's not the end of the world."

Lunchtime in the cafeteria. Amid the rush of students vying to reach the tables before all the good spots were claimed, Pete and D'Andre sat apart from the rest. They hunched over sketch pads in fervent concentration, their elbows jutting to-and-fro as they sought the ideal angles in adding heft to their hieroglyphs. Lined among their lunch bags, arranged in a row from skinniest to fattest, were a rainbow variety of marking pens, the fumes deadening even the liveliest of appetites; hence their unopened meal sacks.

When Pete and D'Andre finally capped their pens, almost in unison, the spectacles gracing their sketchpads provoked nods of mutual respect. Big, sweeping block-letters in Willy Wonka hues; the apexes jutting off in crazy directions and then poking back on themselves to render the words nearly indecipherable to the untrained eye. "EPIC" drawn on one boy's page, "D'RESPECT" on the other.

"Your style's progressing," D'Andre said, eyeing his friend's latest piece. "Really dope lines. And I like how the 'I' here looks like one of those ancient columns we saw in our textbook."

Pete nodded. "Thanks, man. This is awesome, too. Nice faded blend on the colors. You gotta teach me how to do that using just the markers."

D'Andre shrugged. "Takes practice, is all."

They swapped back their pads. Pete flipped through his to trace the artistic progression since the start of the school year: a plethora of rudimentary tags early on in the book, vivid renderings complete with an illusion of three-dimensions gracing the latter pages. For now, only store-bought surfaces laid ground for his art. But D'Andre had mentioned plans of eventually hitting up a certain train yard ripe with mobile canvases.

"And now we eat," D'Andre declared, eyeing his paper bag. "Why you always pack your lunch? I only bring mine on special days."

"Mom cooks big meals," said Pete, "so there's leftovers." He unwrapped a bundle of cellophane containing a square of pastry; layers of crisp, golden phyllo dough sandwiching an ample filling of spinach-and-feta cheese.

"That's the stuff," D'Andre said. "Sp ... *spanakopita*, right?"

Pete smiled. "You know it. When have I ever let you down?" D'Andre went for the spinach pie, but Pete held it out of reach. "Not until you come through with your end."

D'Andre revealed a small Tupperware container, sliding it across the table in exchange for the other snack. Pete popped the lid and eyed the gooey mound of peach cobbler. "That's what I'm talking about!"

"Enjoy," D'Andre muttered, speaking around a mouthful of the savory pastry. "When you gonna have me over for a real Greek dinner?"

"Might be a while. Mom's gonna freak when she sees my braids! I think she'll sorta assume you made me get them. Like a bad influence, y'know?"

D'Andre laughed. "I didn't *make* you get 'em, I just made sure you got 'em done *proper*. Think about it: without your token black friend, you probably would've went to some whiteboy spot, one of those street vendors the hippies use over on Telegraph. They *really* would've fucked your head up. What would your mom say then?"

Pete laughed, too. "No telling. And stop saying you're my 'token black friend,' dammit."

D'Andre spread his palms. "Hey, bro, truth hurts."

Pete rolled his eyes. "Anyway, so you were on point about the class's reaction over my new 'do. Combination of shocked and, weirdly enough, almost angry."

"People pissed that you driftin' over to the dark side, what that is."

"The Outer Limits?" Pete suggested.

"More like your Black Mirror."

Pete chuckled. "Anyway, what did everybody think of your clean-cut look?"

D'Andre gazed up at the ceiling while stroking the peach fuzz on his chin. "Most folks didn't even seem to notice. Nothin' new there, I guess. Being invisible ain't that bad, most of the time."

Pete nibbled at the cobbler to make it last. He felt a subtle shift like the promise of a new understanding that would eventually surface, yet for now remained frustratingly out of reach.

"Matter of fact," D'Andre said now, "you never really did say why you wanted to get braided up all the sudden. Maybe your mom got a right to be a little freaked. I mean, why now?"

Pete tried to conjure an explanation. Then Jordan and Simone, a pair of long-legged, brown-skinned girls—one grade and, for all intents and purposes, an entire world above him—strolled by with a wave. Pete felt his cheeks flush as he returned their greeting.

D'Andre smiled. "How could I not have guessed? Chicks melt for the 'rows, no matter who's rockin' 'em."

"I saw them checking you out, too. See, you're not invisible."

D'Andre chuckled. "That's not how I meant it. The chicks and I always see eye-to-eye."

"How's things with Lisa? Haven't seen you two hanging out in a while."

A shadow passed over D'Andre's face. "We been fighting the last couple nights, ain't talked to her today. Women just get funny with their moods like that sometimes."

At home later that afternoon, Pete's mother stood blocking the doorway, hands-on-hips. Pete would never make it past the big-boned woman without confessing the truth. Hand trembling, he took off the cap. In the initial silence that followed, he sensed his face go pale. He felt younger than his fourteen years; just a kid again, caught in an act of mischief.

"What you do to you hair, for godssakes?" Maria Saropoulos exclaimed, pale-faced.

Pete's cheeks darkened under his mother's gaze—as though her coloring was transferred to him in the act of a cold stare—but he brushed a hand over his tender scalp. "I braided it. Doesn't it look cool?"

"Cool?" His mother parroted, "What this mean 'cool?' Why you did this? Tell me!"

Pete regarded his reflection in the countertop toaster. Only briefly had he checked himself in the mirror that morning, fearing that if he stared too long he would lose his nerve. Now he relished the chance to fully admire his new 'do. If no one else approved of the change, Pete already had D'Andre and his sister Monique's golden seal.

"C'mon, Ma," Pete said, "It's not like I got a tattoo."

Maria quickly crossed herself and muttered, "That's for sure, *doxa toh thiao!*"

"I just felt like trying something different. I'm fourteen now and I can do what I want! I like the way D'Andre has his hair and—"

"You not this boy, don't forget!" Then, addressing him in Greek, his mother said, "I understand you're not a baby anymore, but sometimes you still make very childish decisions. What will the people in church say? And the neighbors? What will your *father* say when he returns home?"

"Ma, I'm not worried about—"

"Me neither because you will go to your room and take those . . . *things* . . ."

Pete marched into his bedroom and slammed the door before his mother could finish.

Freshman year passed in a blur. Pete had yet to kiss a girl, though D'Andre lost his virginity. At the end of that summer, immediately following his sixteenth birthday, D'Andre had reached another milestone in earning a driver's license. While Pete relied on public transit or his own two feet to get around, D'Andre purchased a gleaming, metallic-brown 1979 Chevy Caprice Classic, soon dubbed the "Root Beer Float," with funds he'd claimed to be saving since he was eight-years-old. Pete often found himself riding shotgun to and from school, or in midst of a weekend cruise, lest the passenger seat be occupied by D'Andre's latest love interest, Brittany. With her flawless skin and angel halo of an afro, she was pretty like a portrait from D'Andre's sketchbook.

By sophomore year, Pete's parents green-lighted their son's occasional cruising given that D'Andre had long been absolved for any wrongdoing in influencing Pete to wear braids. Mama had softened to D'Andre the moment he had enthusiastically requested third helpings of her roast chicken and potatoes, while Pete's father beamed upon learning that D'Andre was the budding artist responsible for inspiring his son's creativity.

One Saturday evening in November, D'Andre swooped up Pete from his home with the promise of at last visiting the train yard for that long awaited bombing session. D'Andre kept quiet during the twilight cruise, and not just because of the music pumping through the Chevy's six-by-nines. Though Pete didn't know what to make of his friend's mood, it did seem familiar. More often than not, D'Andre moped through the school halls with his hood up and his hands jammed in his pockets.

Pete gazed out the window at the dull suburban streets. Spray-painted across a bus bench, then again along the side-wall of an auto shop, and a third time—most impressively—way up on a billboard: D'RESPECT, D'Andre's tag, in tones of silver or gold.

As far as Pete knew, D'Andre had shown him all the places he'd hit up in the years prior to their friendship; various alleyways and odd corners throughout the city. But these appeared to be fresh tags. Had D'Andre just been set on solo missions? Or had he not thought Pete ready until now?

When they at last reached the train yard, from the rear seat D'Andre fetched a black hooded sweatshirt, much like the one he so often wore, and handed it to Pete who donned it before following his friend to the trunk. D'Andre brought out a dark plastic bag, its contents rattling around as they approached the fence. Pete almost crashed into D'Andre when he at last bent to examine a portion of chain-link. D'Andre contorted himself through a small hole with seasoned ease. Pete, despite some doubt, followed suit. They crouched side-by-side in dry weeds, their breath materializing in the lithe shapes of spirits set free.

Throughout the yard on sections of track sat the boxcars; steel mastodons immobile on the rails. Their flanks gleamed under the floodlights, coated with elaborate murals in a spray-painted spectrum of colors. Amid the bubble-letter pronouncements stood various figures, some pirated versions of familiar characters: Daffy Duck sporting a gold chain and blood-shot eyes while cradling a giant spliff in one hand and a forty-ounce in another; Charlie Brown offering a defiant frown and a raised middle finger; a topless Jessica Rabbit.

There were also original creations, Pete admiring one in particular: a fairly realistic-looking, pouty-lipped, brown baby wearing a backwards ball cap. The block-lettered piece encased in a thought-bubble above the baby's cap read, 'D'RESPECT!' Pete hadn't noticed a practice-version in D'Andre's sketchbook. He wondered how long it had taken to complete; how many nights D'Andre had stayed out until dawn, laying it down.

They stayed low and out of the light until reaching a boxcar still fairly unadorned. Leaned against the cold steel while regaining his breath, Pete watched D'Andre open the bag to reveal his bounty: ten to fifteen multi-colored cans of Krylon and several spray-nozzle attachments in a variety of widths.

Pete looked to his friend before making a selection as if to be certain he truly had D'Andre's blessing, then snagged a can of gloss-white, which he fitted with a nozzle of the smallest spray-width. His initial painting attempts proved all wrong, the line emerging too thick and drippy, possessing none of the control that accompanied working with markers. He tried again with the same result.

D'Andre came to his aid, demonstrating the proper distance at which to hold the can. After a few more tries, Pete grasped the technique and soon the world fell away.

Finally, he stepped back to briefly marvel at the fine outline of those giant, interlocking, block letters spelling "EPIC." He dove right back in with the black paint, adding a shadow backdrop so the letters seemed to jut off the surface. He returned to the supply bag, eager to add some color, but felt D'Andre's hand on his shoulder. He realized his friend had remained silently in the background the whole time.

"That's probably enough for one session, Pete. Be proud."

Pete cocked his head, noticing for the first time that D'Andre held not a spray can, but a half-empty cognac pint. "How come you didn't paint anything?"

D'Andre took a sip from the bottle, and seemed to contemplate the boxcar. "Kinda seems like kid stuff to me now."

"The fuck are you talking about?" said Pete. "You . . . but I thought…" he let his voice trail as D'Andre gave him a sympathetic glance.

"Think I didn't notice you on the way over peeping all my bombings around town? It's like I got it out of my system. I made my point, left my mark. People forced to acknowledge that, and now I gotta move on."

"Just like that?"

"Yup. There's no chance of turning this graffiti shit into something valuable, bro. All the transplants comin' and taking the legit opportunities. Maybe that mural project I was up for? Damn hipster got it, go figure. Nobody wants art from locals anymore. Shit, the gentrifiers don't even see us."

Pete crossed his arms over his chest. "This isn't you, man! What are you talking about? And when did you start drinking *that* stuff?"

D'Andre gave him a half-smile. "Maybe I been invisible even to you sometimes."

"Aw, don't start with—"

"Brittany broke up with me this morning, dude."

Pete frowned. "Oh. Sorry to hear, but really, so what, right? You'll find another girl. You always do."

"Yeah," D'Andre said, though his voice sounded far away.

Pete, unsure why, felt a ripple of fear. "So," he muttered, "what now?"

D'Andre gazed up at the moon. "Now, we grab a Space Burger."

Pete followed as his friend made toward their hole in the fence.

Pete awoke one Saturday with a good morning text from a Greek girl named Cynthia Papademas. They had been keeping company since the past October, and in turn he and D'Andre hadn't hung out as much.

Hey, handsome, read Cynthia's text, *promised me I could run my hands through those curls soon. When you gonna ditch the braids?*

Pete had alone decided he no longer wanted to wear the cornrows, Cynthia was just the final nudge. Along with his diminished enthusiasm for tagging, he leaned toward a makeover. Time for him to, at least in one respect, grow up.

Rising from bed, he rummaged through the closet and found his sketchpad. He hadn't drawn in months, junior year had almost passed, though the sight of those sketches done back in the lunchroom—his lime green-and-blue raspberry EPIC tag done under D'Andre's critical eye—triggered memories of the train yard expedition. D'Andre had held true to his word to be done with the "kid stuff." Pete had never gone back to complete the mural.

D'Andre, meanwhile, spent a majority of his free time with friends in Richmond. When Pete did meet up with him, something seemed different. D'Andre often talked of his childhood friends and their corner hustles, a subject to which Pete could hardly relate.

Pete, driving his mother's Nissan, didn't even call D'Andre before cruising over. Instead, he dialed D'Andre's sister, Monique, directly to be certain she was free to take out his cornrows. The Bryant family's South Richmond neighborhood always seemed deceptively quiet. Only the sneakers dangling from webs of wire like spider food hinted at illicit activities. Pete couldn't help feel that in rolling through a potentially dangerous place, he was getting away with something.

"Hello, Pete, how are you?" asked D'Andre's mother upon answering the door.

"I'm fine, Missus Bryant, and you?"

"Fine as well. I believe D'Andre's still asleep upstairs, but I can—"

"No, thanks, that's all right," Pete said, though he wondered what kept his friend in bed at eleven o' clock on a bright Saturday morning. "I'm looking for Monique."

Wanda Bryant may have tried to conceal a smile, but Pete couldn't be sure.

"Hey, Pete." Monique sat on a tall stool at the kitchen counter in sweat shorts and tank-top, skimming a magazine and singing softly; the tune unrecognizable, though that hardly mattered.

So taken by the melody, Pete almost forgot to return her greeting. "Hey, Monique."

Monique chuckled, arranging a kitchen chair between her legs. "Come have a seat."

Monique gently tilted Pete's head back, and his sudden proximity to her—the sensation of his neck against her ample thighs—set his heart thudding per usual. At eighteen she was two years older than he, and a year older than D'Andre; not a girl, but a young woman. Pete felt somewhat uncomfortable having a long-standing crush on his best friend's sister, but he had never acted on his feelings.

Monique's fingers massaged the sections of his scalp between each braid. "Sure you want to take these out for good? I mean, I can always redo them later if you change your mind."

Pete hesitated before saying, "I should give my hair a break, let it breathe a while."

"Okay."

Pete closed his eyes and listened to Monique's song, the melody nearly lulling him to sleep. He came alert upon feeling her gently unravel the first braid with the help of a fine-toothed comb.

D'Andre and Monique's father, Derrick, entered in a cream-colored linen walking suit; the man able to pass as D'Andre's twin, were he not twenty-five years his senior. "My baby gon' be a star, don't I know it," he said, running a comb over his crisp, salt-and-pepper fade. "Morning, Pete."

"Hi, Mister Bryant," Pete said, squirming on the stool and feeling his face flush.

Derrick nodded before continuing his declaration. "If only her brother had been blessed with those pipes. Boy and his drawings, I just don't know about all that."

Pete winced at the comment, so unlike those of his own father upon recognizing D'Andre's influence on Pete's artwork: *While some his age can hardly picture their future, my boy can draw his in full-color detail.*

"Good morning to you, too," D'Andre said, strolling into the room. Derrick just snorted, and moved to the fridge. D'Andre turned to Pete. "Yo, man, when you get here?"

Pete squirmed again. "Little while ago. Your mom said you were still in bed, so . . ."

D'Andre stifled a yawn. "Yeah. Out late last night."

"Doin' something less than nothing," Derrick muttered, "and surely up to no good."

D'Andre nodded to his friend instead. "Takin' your 'rows out, I see."

"Feels like the right time," Pete said.

D'Andre regarded Pete with a funny sort of half smile. "Lookin' pretty comfortable in that chair."

Pete's cheeks flushed again.

"You'll be a senior next year, ain't that right, Pete?"

"Yes, sir," Pete replied, thankful Derrick had changed the subject.

"Must have all kinds of plans for after you graduate."

"I am looking at colleges. Might stay close to home, help out Mom and Dad, or . . ." Pete glanced at D'Andre, "might go out of state."

"Got your priorities in order, sounds like."

"Dad, it's Saturday. Pete's probably tired of thinking about this stuff."

"At least he thinks about it, period," Derrick snapped.

Pete breathed deep, wishing Monique would sing again. Far from the first time he had witnessed tension in the Bryant household, though it felt different now; Derrick digging into his son just a little deeper. All the while Monique continued unweaving Pete's braids, her fingers quick and precise.

"My baby girl," Derrick proclaimed, "she'll do this family proud. Not a doubt in my mind."

"Let me know when you're finished, Pete," D'Andre said. Shooting a glance at his father, he added, "I'll be up in my room."

After D'Andre made his exit, Pete closed his eyes; the gentle pressure of Monique's fingertips the only thing that remained, a subtle touch of magic in its own right.

Later that afternoon, Pete and D'Andre strolled the neighborhood that grew shabbier the farther they ventured beyond the Bryant residence. Pete kept running a hand through his unleashed curls, relishing the soothing breeze against his still-tender scalp. Up ahead, a throng of young men paced the street corner, kicking at the pavement, forms rendered larger due to their bulky parkas and dark-colored skull caps despite the weather's warmth. A few sipped from beer cans haphazardly cradled in plastic bags, Pete wondering why they even bothered with the see-through sacks. Unexpected side effects of this return to his old look included curious gazes from passersby. D'Andre had once pointed out that the cornrows, in combination with his Mediterranean complexion, lent Pete a racially ambiguous appearance; a sort of invisibility all its own. Hours ago the neighborhood's residents, by-in-large, might have assumed Pete was of mixed race, and therefore able to blend, at least somewhat, into the crowd. Now he was a strange "whiteboy" in their eyes.

With all eyes on him, Pete expected the worst, though D'Andre only nodded to the group. The men stepped aside to allow access to the liquor store. Pete trailed D'Andre to the magazine rack where he paged through an issue of *Lowrider*. "This the dream car right here," he said, indicating a 1965 Impala SS. "I want this exact color and everything."

"So, you'd sell the Caprice?"

"Probably. I'm talkin' down the road some. Like when I get out the Air Force."

Pete made a face. "Air Force?"

D'Andre closed the magazine. "I'm planning to go into the military after summer."

"Why?"

D'Andre shrugged. "Why not? My grandpops was in the military, figure I continue tradition. We both know school ain't really my thing. I'll get away for a while, earn some money, learn a cool trade, come back, buy my Impala, and be ready for the next step. Whatever it is."

"But why the Air Force?"

"I like the idea of flying planes."

Pete spread his palms. "But you always get on my case when I say I might move away, and now..."

"Look, man, the Air Force is top choice. Who knows, I might just go to the Reserves. If that's the case, I'll still be around. Shit, by that time you might already have a new black friend."

"Stop saying that!"

D'Andre laughed. "Okay, okay. Let's get a drink and go to the park. Sound good?"

"I guess."

"The park" was not much more than a square of dry weeds. Pete and D'Andre sat atop a picnic table to watch the minimal traffic while enjoying their beverages; Pete sipping from a Coke can, D'Andre nursing a fruit-punch flavored wine cooler the color of Windex.

"Does it get on your nerves how your dad always rags on you like that?" Pete asked after they had been sitting in silence for a time. "You can prove him wrong, y'know. You're a great artist. My Dad even says you should go to art school."

"Not an option."

"How come?"

"Not everybody has a dad like yours, ok?"

"... Ok. Why are you drinking so much lately?"

"Quit with the questions. What, are you my mom now?"

Pete didn't answer.

When a young boy cruised up on a bicycle far too big for him, Pete refrained from asking any more questions; staying quiet even as D'Andre produced a baggie of weed from his pocket and traded it for cash. The kid rode away. Pete and D'Andre finished their beverages in silence until D'Andre declared it time to go back.

On a cloudless afternoon in June, a couple months after that fateful Saturday visit to the Bryant residence, Pete sat in the audience as D'Andre graduated high school. When D'Andre posed for a photo on stage beside the principal, Pete hoped, despite how selfish it seemed, his friend would join the Reserves and stay close to home for at least another twelve months until Pete decided whether or not to leave behind everything familiar in beginning his own life quest.

"Congrats, bro," said Pete once D'Andre reached him amid the crowd.

"Thanks, man."

"So, what's next?" Pete asked.

D'Andre's father appeared, "There you are! My son done me proud!" wrapping an arm around his son's shoulder. "Why not sip a lil' something with your old man?" Derrick Bryant swayed on his feet, his eyes a little glassy. From his blazer pocket he withdrew a gin pint and took a swig before passing it to D'Andre, who did the same. When it was his turn, Pete took a courtesy sip.

"Yo, Pete," said D'Andre, "I'm gonna make my rounds. See you tonight?"

Pete nodded. "Tonight it is."

A week after school ended for summer, Pete boarded a Greece-bound plane. When he returned he called D'Andre first thing.

"It's all bad, bro," D'Andre said. "The military is no-go! Fuckers won't let me join 'cause of a 'slight curvature of the spine.' Whatever the hell that means. They found it on my damn pre-enlistment exam."

"Shit, sorry, D—"

"Save it, man. I'm out."

Pete lingered a moment in the silence of the ended call.

His last year at Monte Vista High, it seemed for Pete—by then not even warranting a second look from his fellow students—time passed in a blink. With graduation in sight for the senior class, Pete chose to attend UC Berkeley the next fall, neither he nor D'Andre leaving town in the end. Finally, Pete ran into Monique at the mall in Richmond—the sight of her still quickening his heart. Despite wanting to finally ask her out, in the end he could only muster, "Hey, Monique, looking good! I'm about to graduate." Had he wanted to sound more grown up? Before Pete could try again, Monique spoke.

"That's wonderful, Pete! D'Andre will be so excited for you. He's out in Sacramento now, working at an auto shop and living with a new girlfriend. See you around, Pete."

Pete tried his best to ignore the lump in his throat. "See you."

A week later, a phone call from an unidentified number.

"I want to speak with Pete the Greek!"

"D'Andre?"

"Well, duh. What you been up to, my brother from a Mediterranean mother?"

"The UC Berkeley grind, is all. How you doing? Man, I had no way to contact you. How'd you get my cell?"

"What you think, bro? Monique! I'm back in the Bay, living in Oakland now, working security again. We gotta hook up soon.'"

"Definitely."

The friends met in Berkeley for dinner at Kip's Bar and Grill. Pete arrived first, and when D'Andre at last entered the restaurant it took Pete a moment to recognize him; his old buddy thinner than he remembered, eyes heavy-lidded and red-rimmed. But D'Andre's signature smile, the one that seemed to require the participation of his entire face, remained as bright as it had when they were teenagers.

"Get up and give me a hug, partner!"

"Good to see you," Pete replied. "I thought you'd disappeared."

"Shit, I up and did for a good while. But you wouldn't have wanted to hear from me couple years back. I wasn't in the best place."

"How so?"

"Man, just problems with me and my old lady." D'Andre skimmed the menu. "They got good beers on tap here, I'm gonna start with one of them."

After their meals arrived, D'Andre merely picked at his burger, though he drained two pints of beer and didn't hesitate in ordering a third, even while Pete still nursed his first.

"Say, bro, I hate to ask and all," D'Andre began, "but you think I could borrow some money?

Pete felt his palms go slightly damp as he clasped and unclasped his hands.

"Sorry to put you on the spot, especially after it's been so long, except these fools at the job are always playin' with my check! Promise I'll pay you back. With interest even."

"Sure. How much do you need?"

D'Andre dropped his gaze. "A hundred, if you can spare it. I can cover the rest of my bills, and, like I mentioned before, I'll repay you with interest."

"I can swing that."

"Thanks! It really helps."

Pete smiled. "That's what brothers are for, right?"

"No doubt."

The following weekend, Pete recovered his loan with interest as promised. He and D'Andre spent Saturday afternoon at the hoop courts, laughing and talking shit like old times. D'Andre even paid for a late lunch at Jack London Square, though Pete felt a little uneasy when D'Andre started drinking. Between cocktail after cocktail D'Andre recounted the many break-up-make-up cycles with his current girlfriend. Upon finishing their meal, D'Andre was so unsteady on his feet that Pete had to help him out the door.

As they reached the car, D'Andre met Pete's eyes. "My girl is pregnant. She's gonna have another baby and I think her ex, the father of her two girls, is the dad. Not me."

"Shit. Are you sure?"

D'Andre handed his cell phone to Pete. "Hold onto this. I don't want it."

"What are you talking about?"

"She's gonna call me and I don't want to talk to her." He stumbled up the block, and Pete jogged to catch him.

"You're really drunk, bro," he said. "You're not making sense. Let's go back to the car. You can crash at my place and we'll talk about this in the morning. Deal?"

"Okay," D'Andre breathed, "deal."

Two weeks passed before D'Andre phoned in need of another loan, claiming to have been let go from his job. Pete, suspicious of how the cash was being spent and not wanting to fund his friend's drinking habit, hesitated in lending more money but ultimately gave in. When D'Andre showed up at his door to accept the favor, he arrived with a pair of younger guys; shifty-eyed characters who kept their heads down as if unworthy of greeting. The sharp tang of bammer wafted off them and they looked like they wanted to be anywhere but standing on his porch. D'Andre seemed, for some reason, self-conscious in their presence. He refrained from flashing his signature smile when greeting Pete, saying little and appearing in a rush as he received the loan. Then he retreated back down the steps toward his car with the two strangers in tow.

A month later, Pete heard a familiar voice as he strolled the waterfront along Jack London Square.

"You shoppin' for boats as well?"

D'Andre stood waving from the edge of the docks, his form backlit by the setting sun like a hazy apparition in the waning dusk. Pete just stood as if unsure of the vision's reality.

"Well, come on, man!" D'Andre called out again. "You can get a better view from over here."

"What're you doing out this way?"

"Same as you, I guess," D'Andre responded with a smile, "takin' in the sights. How you been?"

"Same old."

D'Andre nodded. "I'm gonna get you that money back, I promise."

"Aw, don't worry about it."

"No, seriously. I'm still in transition with the job, but as soon as I get on my feet . . ."

"Thanks, dude. No rush. Anyway, how are *you*? I've been calling, texting, and no response. Feel like a sucker chasing a girl who keeps leaving my messages on 'read.'"

D'Andre laughed, then gazed out at the horizon. "Speaking of, me and ol' girl are taking a little break. We're not *broken* up, but . . . anyway, still haven't found out whether or not the baby is mine." He indicated a mid-size yacht named *The Thelma Jane*. "I got my eye on that one. Maybe we can sail the Greek isles some day."

Pete smiled. "Sounds like a plan. Good seeing you. I need to get on. Study time for a big exam tomorrow."

"Hey, no thing," said D'Andre, "I'll be in touch."

Pete couldn't grasp why his friend had often gone through the trouble of making a spectacle of himself only to vanish over and over again. Pete slowly resigned to the fact that there was no looking for someone who didn't want to be found.

WINTER
XEIMΩNA
2013

After
care

That morning, for the first time in over three weeks, he awoke thinking of his ex Courtney. He'd been the one to break things off after her constant talk of wanting children left him feeling suffocated. Now he wanted to hear her voice. But the voice he needed to hear belonged to Alex who had a lead on a new job. They were due to meet up, and Mike was already running late.

At the coffee shop, Alex had claimed an outdoor spot and sat hunched forward in his chair, looking ready to pounce into his pitch about the work opportunity. Instead, upon seeing Mike, he leaned back and crossed his arms over his chest. "Tell me you didn't call her."

Mike sighed while settling into his chair. "No, but I wanted to."

"You gotta let her go."

"Now you tell me."

Alex, somehow amid masterminding behind-the-scenes of the food truck operation, had met Courtney. He apparently felt that, with her buoyant personality and vivid green eyes, Courtney was a good fit for Mike. Alex hosted them for dinner one night. Over fancy takeout, Mike offered to take Courtney out somewhere fancy. They fell for each other fast, and before long Courtney was probing his feelings about starting a family.

"So," Alex began as Mike returned to the table after grabbing a beverage, "I know you've been out of work since the bar closed, and I'm thinking why not try something totally different…"

Mike tuned out as a guy passed pushing a stroller. The baby had a perfectly round face, and a thoughtful expression emphasized by brows like smoky suggestions above huge brown eyes that appeared to miss nothing. The infant even smiled as they went by. In turning back toward his friend, Mike said, "You think it's strange to suddenly have this desire to be a father? Especially after not wanting that at all?"

Alex made a face. "Were you listening? I just finished telling you about—"

"I'm serious, man. Humor me."

"Ok," Alex said in regard to Mike's admission. "That does sound a little weird."

"But what could have brought it on?"

"I don't know. Except I'm what, ten years younger than you? I can't imagine being one-hundred percent committed to a woman right now, much less having a *kid*, but who knows, when I'm thirty-four I'll probably feel different."

"You think so?"

Alex shrugged. "Sure. Kids are cool, from a distance, usually. If anyone's going to make you feel like a weirdo for being a man who cares about children, and is interested in having his own, then that says something about their own perverted mindset. Plus, it's not like you've never been around children before. When our families traveled back to Greece together, you even saved those tourist kids on the beach."

"I never really gave that much thought."

Alex shrugged again. "So, maybe this new desire isn't so new after all. Maybe you're just aware of it in a different way."

Mike narrowed his eyes in contemplation. "Maybe it reminds me of something from the past."

"There you go," Alex said. "Think back to when you were in school. How many of your teachers were guys? Not many in my case. Young boys need role models just like young girls, right? If you're still looking for that second job, why not work with kids?"

Mike cocked his head. "Like at a group home or something?"

"If you'd been listening, you'd know I've got a friend who runs the After School Program at a private elementary up in the hills. You have some experience tutoring, right?"

"That was a long time ago."

"Just apply for the job! It might give you some added perspective."

"That's actually a great idea!"

"As usual, right?"

Four days later, Mike had an interview for the After School Staff position at Ohlone Academy. But that particular morning, as he rose from bed and got in the shower, work was not the first thing on his mind. He recalled how early on in dating Courtney there had been a few occasions when he had recognized her ability to halt time. A subtle magic she possessed, evident in the way she cocked her head slightly to one side when she smiled, and in how she brushed her hair behind her ear in moments of contemplation. During those instances, time seemed to stop, and for a few seconds Mike had pictured her as someone with whom he could settle down. But she proved unable to maintain those moments of suspended animation compared to those in which he felt claustrophobic in her company.

Now, with the warm water streaming over his head, Mike wondered how many times he'd used *claustrophobia*—a Greek word, after all—as an excuse to let women go when they couldn't maintain the magic. Never mind that he had probably been lazy in doing his part. For the first time, he considered that had he been more patient, he may have learned that Courtney was a perfect mother to a child, *their* child, something he may have subconsciously wanted with her all along. It seemed ironic that in the weeks before their break-up, they had made love with greater frequency than at any time prior, their bodies joined in a constant frenzy of tangled sheets. Sex had seemingly become their sole method of communication— the activity in which they could exert both tenderness and aggression without having to justify themselves to one another.

In the car he felt a little better, despite taking a series of wrong turns up windy lanes lined with golden grass almost the same color as the fire it seemed to invite, and extravagant, multiple-story homes with windows reflecting the sun-dappled Bay as it shimmered in the distance.

At last, he located Ohlone Academy. With the Fall session nearing winter break, most students were in class at this hour, but as he traversed the blacktop a mother and father walked with their kindergartener, the child holding their hands and swinging between them while they crossed the playground amid early dismissal for young grades.

"You must be Mike Lagounis? I'm Corrine Alvarado. Nice meeting you."

Mike took the hand of Ms. Alvarado, a well-dressed, brown-skinned woman of short stature and bright smile, and returned her greeting before following her into the teacher's lounge. She offered him a coffee and a seat at a round table covered by cloth patterned with colorful illustrations of books and pencils.

"Alex has told me great things," she said, pulling up a chair across from him, "namely that you have saved more than one child drowning in the sea? That's quite the accomplishment."

Mike hesitated. Then it dawned on him that Alex must have, in his usual fashion, exaggerated the story so that it's all-too-average protagonist seemed a man capable of Herculean heroics. In reality, during that trip to Greece, Mike had led a pair of tourist children back to the beach shore after they panicked when a current carried them out to the depths. In their fear they had certainly thrashed about—not exactly *drowning*—but that had been the only such episode. Still, Mike cleared his throat and said, "Nothing major."

Ms. Alvarado smiled. "I'm impressed by your modesty. Anyhow, I can't say you'll be called upon in this job to respond to such drastic situations, but it's great to know you're capable in an emergency. The most you'll have to deal with here is an occasional skirmish, but even those are rare. At Ohlone, we have zero-tolerance for bullying, and we seldom see problems with children fighting. Now, let's see, according to your resume you are currently employed nightly at a bar?"

"I was. The spot just closed, another casualty of rising rents."

"What inspired you to get into work with kids as an After School Program Instructor?"

"I've just had this feeling lately that, to me personally, children are really important."

"Do you have any of your own?"

"Not currently."

"But you'd like to have some."

Mike shifted in his seat. "Someday. Yes."

"It's wonderful to be in the position of considering a male addition to our staff. Men are nurturers, too, after all."

On the drive home, Mike kept replaying what Ms. Alvarado had said about prospective male employees, the way her view had gone against Alex's stance.

The next day when awakened by the phone, he almost didn't pick up in time.

"Mike? It's Missus Alvarado. I'm thrilled to offer you the After School Program Instructor position with Ohlone Elementary!"

Mike rubbed his eyes and tried to muster as much enthusiasm as possible given his fatigue. "That's great . . . thanks. Thank you so much!"

"I look forward to seeing you later today then."

"Today?"

"Yes, unless that's a problem? This is a rush hire, and your background check has already cleared."

"Sounds good, Missus Alvarado. See you soon."

At two-thirty that afternoon, he arrived for work struck by the contrast compared to his first time on campus. Children everywhere: little kids and big kids milling about between classes, anticipating the day's dismissal as they shouted at one another, their laughter and gleeful screams echoing among the portables like those red rubber balls that were bounced during recess. Despite knowing the age group with whom he'd be working, Mike realized that he had still been envisioning babies.

As he made his way toward the building, a boy of about nine-years-old nearly knocked him over as he came galloping around the corner. In all his sudden desire to have a child with someone, not once had Mike considered that an infant would soon grow into a perpetually-hungry whirlwind like the one who had just hurricaned past.

The After-Care Room was stocked with "no-mess" tile floors, plastic tables and chairs, multi-colored bean-bag sofas, and an abundance of toys, board games, and craft supplies. Mike was again greeted by Ms. Alvarado, and then re-introduced to his co-workers whom he had met briefly at the morning orientation. Of the eight staff members on the after-school team, Mike included, there was only one other male, a veteran to the job named Chuck—or Mr. Lawrence to the students—who looked at least ten years Mike's senior.

"First day jitters?" Chuck asked.

Mike wiped his palms on his slacks and said, "A few."

"No need to be nervous. Just be kind, but firm. Don't be afraid to send someone to the office if they get too rowdy."

Mike was stationed in the library where, aside from general supervision, he was given the task of helping students with homework and assuring that the noise-levels remained low. That sounded simpler than it proved as in the time it had taken to trek the ten feet over from the After-Care Room, the space had already filled with kids, a mish-mash of first through sixth graders, conversing at a pitch level that defied reason.

Mike glanced over at the librarian's desk in hopes of finding some reinforcement, but she had already left for the day and he couldn't blame her. So he just stood there for a long moment amidst the chaos. The kids who happened to notice him went right on causing havoc. At the old bar, when things got too unruly they had cut the music and . . . *that was it!* An idea so simple, yet hopefully effective. He switched off the lights, and momentarily cranked the radio until the sounds of those children who had remained unfazed by the sudden darkness were drowned out by the classical symphony blaring through the speakers.

"Okay, now that I've got everyone's attention," he said after killing the radio and turning the lights back on, "I want to introduce myself as Mister Lagounis and inform you that it's homework time in the library. That means for the next hour I expect you to work *quietly*. No video games on the computers. Only school stuff. And, if you don't have homework right now, well, the great thing about being in a library is that you're surrounded by *books*. And if you still can't handle reading or doing homework *quietly*, you're more than welcomed to play on the yard. Understood?"

Mike relished the captured attention. He assumed that he'd earned a clear victory. But then the noise resumed at an only slightly more tolerable level. At least the video games were abandoned.

"Mister Lagounis. Mister Lagounis?"

Mike found a student beside him, third or fourth grade. "Hi," Mike said, "how can I help you?"

"Come see," exclaimed the wide-eyed girl.

She grabbed his hand, almost dragging Mike around a partition into the "Children's Section," where he spied two boys crouched over a spread-eagle Minnie Mouse doll, it's skirt yanked up and a Lincoln Log jammed in its crotch.

"You two!" Mike roared. "The office! *Now!*"

After finding someone to cover for him, Mike hurried to the office where the boys sat with hanging heads before Ms. Alvardo's desk. The expression on the Program Director's face, as she regarded them from her chair with arms crossed over chest, was enough to make Mike wince.

Ms. Alvarado greeted him, and then requested his version of the story before asking the boys whether or not they understood the wrongfulness in their actions. As they muttered something about how they felt bad for "destroying school property," Mike could no longer hold back what he felt needed to be said.

"Listen, guys, it's not just that you ripped the doll, understand?" The pair gazed up at him with big eyes and down-turned lips, but he wasn't going to let them off easy. "Maybe you weren't thinking about what you were doing, but the fact that it's a female doll, and you flipped her skirt up and shoved something into her like that . . ."

"But," one of the boy's whimpered, "it's just a doll of a *mouse*."

Mike's posture now mirrored Ms. Alvarado's. "It doesn't matter, and this isn't a joke! As young men you have to know what's appropriate, and you did what you did in front of a young female student. Think about how that might've made her feel."

The boys hung their heads again, and Mike felt his point was made. Later, Ms. Alvarado caught up to him as he was en-route to the playground for yard duty. "I'm really happy with how you handled the situation with those boys, Mister Lagounis. You brought up an important point, and did so with firmness and sensitivity. Our male students need strong role models and they're lucky to have you on the staff. I think you'll make a great father someday."

Mike smiled. "Thank you."

That night he treated himself to dinner out, and quietly beamed over his first day heroics as an After School Program Instructor. Midway through his meal, the phone rang. Mike reached into his pocket, cursing under his breath. Fellow diners, enjoying their tacos and burritos, frowned at him as his ringtone went on jingling. As Mike finally freed his phone, his eyebrows jumped at the name flashing across its screen.

"Hey, Courtney," Mike said, trying to sound nonchalant. "What's up?"

"Oh . . . quite a bit, actually," said Courtney.

A pause, and Mike thought he'd detected a slight tremor in Courtney's voice. "You okay?"

"Well, I didn't want to say this over the phone. But it's obviously been a while since we've seen each other, and that might be more awkward, so . . . I'm pregnant, Mike."

"You're absolutely sure?"

"Yes."

"And..."

"Yes, Mike, it's yours. I haven't slept with anyone since you, and you know we weren't always careful. I don't know what I'm gonna do."

"I don't know," said Mike, trying to steel his voice. "But we'll figure it out. Together."

"You're not mad?"

"Of course not! This could be a really good thing, actually."

Courtney didn't respond, but Mike sensed her smile, however small, on the other line.

High
note

At thirty-four, Johnny Eliopoulos had spent countless evenings in venues such as this dimly-lit lounge where the reek of liquor and sweat wafted, and tobacco clouds hung thick as gauze despite No Smoking laws. Now, however, on one hand without even using all five fingers he could count the number of such venues remaining in Oakland. One by one the Town's live blues and soul music clubs were replaced by shiny night spots where DJ-provided electro-pop synthesizers made singer-songwriters obsolete. So, on the ever-rarer occasion when Johnny got the opportunity to perform, he knew to make the most of his high notes.

Tonight was one of those nights. He rippled his fingers across his piano keys. When he crooned the first line, women—as though appearing from the ether—swarmed the stage; a looming tsunami of brunettes, blondes, and redheads. The sight of such a multitude caused his voice to flutter as he hoped he hadn't forgotten how to swim.

Johnny had dedicated more than half his life to perfecting this magic trick; a sure-fire spell, and the one thing that made worthwhile all those years spent practicing piano and refining his voice. In high school and college he had wowed even the most skeptical of his friends while performing various classic soul ballads: black music from bygone eras of which he had little reference, though he loved the tunes just the same. Soon, it seemed, he would need every bit of magic to muster up a following before his dream evaporated.

Backstage after the show, he sat at a table counting his tips. Meanwhile his friend, Mike Lagounis, tallied non-monetary earnings. "Wow, brother, let's see. You got five business cards, six napkins, and four gum wrappers. I'd say it was a good night. Who you gonna call first?"

Johnny sipped bourbon to balance the post-performance endorphin blast. "I don't know, brother, might not call any."

Mike laughed. "Because you already have so many waiting in the wings? Don't take this wrong, but your life is *such* a cliché. The journeyman singer-songwriter playing the dying lounge scene, falling asleep next to a new woman every night. Good luck getting a movie deal based on that bio. At least you're Greek. That's somewhat unique. Aren't too many Greek-American soul singers."

Johnny laughed, too. Not the first time someone had told him he was living a stereotype. "You've got a hell of a way of telling me my luck is running out. Okay, how's this for unique? I've gone celibate."

"What's the occasion?"

"*Celibate*, you idiot."

"What? For a second I thought you were serious."

"I am."

"Shit, are you sick or something?"

Johnny waved him off. "No, but I am sick of these women only wanting me for one thing. Every time I meet someone things are great until they come out and say they're just interested in sleeping with me."

Mike chuckled. "The world should have your problems, man. Meanwhile, this club is about to become another Jumping Acorn."

"Wish I could save the soul scene, but I'm powerless. Maybe with all the time freed up by my sex strike I can at least save my cashflow."

"Thinking about getting another gig?"

"Might have to."

"You sounded sexy up there, I mean it."

They turned to find a woman in the doorway.

With a smirk, Mike said, "Backstage pass?"

"What?" the woman asked.

"Nothing," said Mike, chuckling. "I'll give you all some privacy."

When they were alone, the woman extended her hand. "I'm Laura, by the way."

"Nice necklace, Laura," Johnny said. "Is that an emerald? I'm a Taurus, too."

Laura smiled. "Maybe we're a match meant to be. Can I buy you a drink?"

"You know, I'm about to head out."

Gazing at him with heavy-lidded eyes, Laura slid her fingers into his belt loops. "Can I come along?"

"I don't know what more there is to do tonight."

"I'm sure we can come up with a few things."

Well, here goes. "You might not believe this, but I'm practicing celibacy."

Laura let go of his waist, chuckled, and then remarked, "That's actually a great line. Make the woman feel like she has to call your bluff. So, when did you take the vows?"

"This morning."

Laura stepped back and raised her eyebrows. "You're serious, aren't you?"

"Yes."

"Poor baby. You must be having *such* a hard time. So what's the reason for the self-denial?"

Johnny adjusted his trousers. "You're an attractive woman, and a lot of the time you must feel like men are only interested in what you look like. Believe it or not, I know how that is, only in reverse. For once I want to build a mental connection before the physical."

Laura crossed her arms. "Fair enough. So, what do you have to say?"

"Hmm?"

"What do you have to say that you want women to hear?"

Johnny eyed the piano's refuge beyond his reach. "Well, it's not like I just want to stand around talking at them. I want meaningful conversation."

"Okay, so start one."

"What brought you out tonight?"

"But that's about *me*, say something about *you*."

Johnny indicated the piano. "Up there I'm a magician. The audience may not realize it's under a spell, but when I press the keys accordingly, a little harder here, a little softer there, I can see the notes like shifting colors."

"Mmm, the *piano man*. Like that old song. That was certainly poetic, romantic, just like your lyrics. But I'd suggest you ease into the introspective revelations with a little small talk. Women like it."

"And I've never been good at it."

"Practice is all it takes." Laura offered a card with 'DATE-A-DANDY' inscribed on the front. "That's a service that allows women to 'rent' a gentleman for the day. The man is at their beck and whim: taking them to dinner, wine tasting, even cleaning their house or doing handy work if that's what the client desires. A woman might even ask a guy to serenade her assuming it's in his skill set."

Johnny studied the card. "An escort service?"

"Unlike an escort service, no sex allowed. Not even kissing. My sister's the CEO and she pays her gents quite well, so if you're in need of some extra cash you might consider putting in an application."

Johnny pocketed the card. "Thanks, I guess."

Laura smiled. "Now back to your celibacy thing. Does that mean kissing is off limits too?"

"No. I guess not..."

Before he realized it, Laura's lips had met his. She was a good kisser, and so he went with it. But he only felt foolish in the aftermath, knowing he lacked the resolve to stick to his plan for even a full day.

His next scheduled performance, a weekly gig, was a bust due to the venue's looming closure. A week passed. Seven days without sex wasn't so bad after all. By day fourteen, however, the lack of female company and the absence of income had him pondering the DATE-A-DANDY business card. He scored an interview where, after answering standard background questions, he was asked to showcase his musical talents. He sang Levert's 1987 R&B hit "Casanova," and sure enough by song's end every woman in the room was on the edge of her seat. He accepted the work offer of fifty dollars an hour, and three days later was booked by his first client, Denise, a forty-one-year-old divorced mother of two. Upon her request they met at a coffee shop near Lake Merritt. Johnny arrived first and shortly thereafter was greeted by a fit brunette in shorts-and-tank-top.

"So, you're a singer-songwriter?" asked Denise.

"Yeah, I was briefly signed to a major label in my early twenties, but never released an album. Now, with all the newcomers, Oakland wants a different sound. I can hardly find a place to play."

"Just from that clip on the website, I can tell you've got quite the voice. You can definitely play for me."

"Thanks. So, you're actually my first client. What brings you to the service? I find it hard to believe that such an attractive woman would have difficulty landing a date."

"I was married for a long time and just want to enjoy some gentlemanly company without the usual expectations. And why does a handsome young man such as yourself seek this line of work?"

"I've always been a pretty quiet guy, but women dig the—"

"'Man-of-mystery' vibe?"

Johnny laughed. "Exactly. The singing never hurts, either. Anyway, this situation gives me a chance to enjoy female company without, as you said, the usual expectations. Plus, like you mentioned, I may have just found a new way to showcase my music."

Denise sipped her coffee. "So, you're Greek, right?"

"I was born here, but yeah, my background is Greek."

"I'd imagine a lot of women want the 'Mediterranean lover' experience."

"That's been the case more than once. The stereotype's hard to live up to sometimes."

"Well, cheers to a date free of presumptuous expectations."

They spent the remainder of the afternoon walking the lake and chatting, arm-in-arm. On more than one occasion, when their eyes met, Johnny resisted the temptation to kiss Denise. He took pride in playing by the rules. But then Denise, childless for the weekend, asked him over to her apartment.

"Is that allowed, or should I recheck the rulebook?" Johnny asked.

Denise smiled. "Of course it's allowed, even encouraged."

Johnny smiled, too, albeit cautiously. "If you say so."

At home with Denise, Johnny noticed a piano. "Do you play?"

"No, my ex-husband did play professionally when we were still in LA. He's a bar owner now, but I think he'd relate to your plight."

Denise claimed a seat on the couch, crossed her shapely legs, and then made a forbidding wagging motion with her finger when Johnny went to sit beside her.

"Please, no," she said. "Just remain standing, if you don't mind. I just want to look at you for a moment."

Johnny cleared his throat and did as told. Upon further glance, beach-themed nicknacks—a conch shell shimmering its iridescence atop the piano; a splatter-painted surfboard hanging on the wall like art; a miniature faux palm tree positioned like a house plant—accented the decor as if the former couple had wanted to bring SoCal up north.

"You are so very handsome," Denise said after a time, "and have this indescribable swagger when you walk. I've never had such a hot-blooded, Mediterranean . . . fold my laundry."

"What?"

"I'd like you to fold my laundry, please. The washer-dryer is in the kitchen, right down the hall. After you're done you can cook me dinner . . . since your profile boasts your musical *and* culinary skills. "

Johnny was a little surprised, but the request was legit. She followed him into the kitchen to watch as he unloaded the dryer.

"Take your shirt off, please."

Once again, Johnny did as told. Normally, he might have been tempted to flex, but now he only felt silly. When the laundry was done, he asked what Denise wanted for dinner. Per request, he prepared a double-portion of filet salmon. Dinner served, Johnny was permitted to re-don his shirt, and join Denise for a pleasant meal. They talked of their families, hobbies, and even politics. After, Johnny washed the dishes.

"You've been a perfect gentleman," Denise said. "Would you sing me a song before we part?"

Johnny hesitated, and then asked, "What's your pleasure?"

"How about some Stevie Wonder. *My Cherie Amore?*"

"Certainly." Johnny sang the tune while watching Denise's eyes shimmer.

"If you want to break the rules," she said, after he had finished, "I'll pay extra."

Johnny sighed. "I've ... actually taken a vow of celibacy."

Denise chuckled. "That's a good one! Ever the gentleman. I bet my ex would hire you as a regular feature at his bar. I'll talk to him."

Despite an initial leap of his heart, Johnny tempered his enthusiasm. "One of the new spots crowding out old turf?"

"Yes. But he's committed to keeping an Oakland flair. His staff is entirely made up of neighborhood locals."

"I like the sound of that," said Johnny. He could admit that this first gig seemed to be ending on a high note; one that could prolong itself and even inspire new songs. "How can I repay you for the offer?"

Denise touched her lip. "How about an encore performance of an original ballad?"

Johnny's smile widened in preparation to sing. "Good deal."

Broken
glaSS

Dear Little One,

The thought of you is enough to warm this December night. Oakland winters are mild, so say the transplants from the Midwest and East Coast. Sensations of "hot" and "cold" are relative. I say the chill hits deeper when we're alone. Your mother loved to cuddle. Now I can't remember the last time I held her. "Hot" and "cold;" "love" and "heartbreak"—these are words you'll learn soon enough. If only rescuing you from an unhappy love affair was as easy as telling you to come inside when temperatures drop.

I can't wait for us to finally meet. You're the one thing I've done right, I can already tell. Just having you here—just you being *you*—will make up for all my mistakes. Get a load of this one: brick through a window. A stupid thing to do, but I did it.

You don't know me yet. I've never been a bully, never been in trouble with the law. My name's Mike Lagounis. That's *La-goo-nis*, as someday you'll pronounce it for your non-Greek friends. They'll smile, just like you will while reading this letter. I'm your father. Or at least I will be soon.

Your grandparents divorced when I was in high school. But I wasn't a troubled teen, even though my life was uprooted when Mom and I moved out of the red house near Lake Merritt where I'd grown up. We settled in an apartment in Hercules. I didn't see much of Dad for a while. He was busy with work. I gave him space. We talked on the phone, and wrote letters, just like I'm writing to you now. Anyway, Hercules wasn't exactly suburbia. But to fifteen-year-old me, it had a small-town feel compared to Oakland. Yeah, *that* Oakland, the West Coast's answer to Brooklyn, apparently. The new hipster Mecca these days. My city will soon be yours. Can't get more Oakland than a birth at Kaiser, yep, the same hospital where I was born is the one we chose to welcome you.

We locals try to catch our breath as our city breathes anew, as the Town groans and whines its growing pains just loud enough for us to hear. New businesses crowd out older establishments as they sprout up like teeth through tender gums. It's not that we're pissed about it. Call us amused. Maybe overwhelmed is how we feel. Change isn't always easy, but let me quit preaching and reminisce instead.

I know something about the makeover a city has as its demographics shift. As a kid, in the mid-'80's, at four or five-years-old, I'd often spend weekends at the home of my *yiayia*—my father's mother, your *great* grandmother! An immigrant from Sparta, Yiayia arrived in the States as a teenager in 1925 to join her already established older brother in West Oakland's bustling Greek community. The family lived right above the candy shop my great-grandfather owned on the corner of 8th and Castro streets. What I'm saying is that while my family also came to Oakland from someplace else, we were here long before it was a destination.

Anyway, from Yiayia's house I would walk to the corner on Saturday afternoons, my hand in hers as we boarded the 51 bus, my feet sticking straight out from the edge of the seat while we cruised Broadway to downtown. I'd notice the tall buildings; the few skyscrapers. Yiayia would point out the small indie grocers and shoe-shine huts, then she'd talk about all the boarded-up storefronts. Most people didn't go downtown on weekends unless they were, like us, headed to the department stores. Back then, most of the bus passengers were black.

Now, I bet you're wondering what this has to do with me pitching a brick, but it'll all tie together.

So, baby, I've been back in Oakland for about a year now. I left as a kid, came back as a man. Just wait, you'll grow up so fast. But not faster than these changes in the Town. I stroll 19th and think, 'Where did all the white people come from?' This once chocolate city has been vanilla-fied by Pabst-chugging twenty-somethings rushing in from wherever the hell Hipsterland actually is. You'll see what I mean, little one, soon enough.

No more boarded-up buildings like I remember as a child. Now there's trendy cafes and cocktail lounges of shiny steel and polished glass. Over-priced eateries. Even a few mega-chain stores have invaded. None of this really bothered me at first. Things change, people change, places change.

But after shuffling around a while among the ranks of the local-and-jobless, I finally got a gig working at the bar of an older dive called The White Fang down on Broadway near Jack London Square. After I got the call, in celebration, I decided to hit up another classic spot, a little blues club on the same block. Or so I thought. I prowled the street that evening, side-stepping the oddly-mixed throng of well-dressed young professionals and grungy, biker-gang-looking-dudes.

Startled, I retraced my steps. In place of The Jumping Acorn—with its low ceilings and dim light, its cognac-stained leather couches by the tiny stage where John Lee Hooker, Tower of Power, and lesser known local blues and soul acts had performed—stood a posh new restaurant. The kind of place that boasted panoramic windows giving view of the well-dressed, mostly white diners sitting at their linen-clothed tables sipping wine and devouring high-end slabs of meat, their jaw muscles flexing with each showy bite.

I stood in the doorway of "Sustenance" so long that a young, blonde hostess finally came out and asked—no, *inquired*—if I wanted to see a menu. I nodded my head and claimed a spot at the bar counter. The space featured the same low ceiling, and I could vaguely place where the stage had been. But there was no history on those walls, just white paint concealing every past shade. I was further surprised by the restaurant's clientele: men and women of a variety of ethnicities, though they all seemed to fall into two basic categories; hipsters or white-collar professionals. Definitely not the blue-collar crowd of old. You, little one, can wear whatever color collar you choose. I hope by that time there's a trace left of the real Oakland, or else you'll only have this letter as proof the true Town ever existed.

Anyway, at around ten o' clock, a black gentleman in his sixties strode in wearing a leather jacket and a rakish fedora. I didn't immediately recognize the gentleman until he took off his hat and smiled.

"Mikey, is that you?"

"Charles! Man, it's been a while. I'm so sorry about what happened here. The club..."

Brown and creased as baseball gloves, Charles spread his large hands on the counter, his pinkie ring glinting beneath the lamps. "I appreciate your condolences, buddy. Restaurant owner who moved in tried to throw me a bone. Heard about my catfish fry and wanted to know if I'd come in a couple nights and cook it for him. You know, officially put it on the menu like? Not before they fancied it up a whole bunch, of course. I said thank you, sir, but no thanks. That catfish was meant for Sunday dinners with a side of blues, not a splash of 'lemon-garlic aioli' or '*shoe string pomme frites*' like he was talkin'." Charles had one of those voices that seemed to come from an old radio; its scratchy bass pitch carrying the faintest echo.

"I'm about done with the grieving, though. Mourn something too long and you'll die right along with it."

Beside us a waiter appeared. "You gentlemen ready to order?"

"Not just yet, thanks." Then, on some kind of impulse, I asked, "Is the owner here?"

The waiter frowned. "Excuse me? Sir, the owner has his priorities. He doesn't just come out and chat with anyone."

With a smile, I said, "But I'm not just anyone. I'm a true Oaklander."

The waiter raised an eyebrow. "Maybe in that case . . . the owner does always say he's waiting to meet a native. I'll check if he's free."

Before I could change my mind, he was gone. Charles fiddled with his ring. I scanned the top-shelf liquor.

A pony-tailed man in his late forties materialized at my elbow. "Hello, sir," he said. "As you can see, things are pretty busy. How can I help you?"

Isn't that how it always is lately? Everyone trying to help. Then I said, "I . . . I'm a long time Oakland resident, and just wanted to welcome you to the city."

He simply smiled. "So, you're one of those people who remember this place like it used to be."

I wasn't sure what he meant by that. I'm still not sure. Then, Charles's voice sounded a sudden boom.

"Damn right we remember it! This used to be my spot . . . the club was my life!"

The restaurant owner took a step back. "Calm down, sir."

"Don't tell me how to be, youngster!"

My temples began to pound.

"Sir, I'm going to have to call the police . . ."

I took a deep breath as months old news footage of Victor Jameson's death played in my mind. "Don't go through the trouble, asshole!" I barked at the owner. "We're just leaving."

In following Charles toward the exit, I took a glance over my shoulder in time to catch the owner's smirk. "Enjoy your evening! Next time buy something, huh? And tell the other natives!"

Stepping out, I held the door for a young couple. The man said to the woman, "This place looks like a taste of real Oakland."

Right then, discarded in the gutter as a relic from that time when things were different, I spotted the brick. Nobody hurt, little one. Just broken glass. It was a bad night, we all have those. It's a hard time in the Town. But when you get here, things will get better ... maybe a little like how they used to be, back when everyone was welcome. That's the Town that awaits; new to you but old to me.

SPRING
ΑΝΟΙΞΗ
2014

Nine
-to-five

In 1989, four weeks after his arrival from Greece, twenty-five-year-old Dino Kouros knew little of American television. No surprise that when his boss made reference to a popular primetime sitcom, Dino could only smile from atop the ladder while squinting against the sun.

"We might be in some trouble, Dino," said Mr. Phillips, gazing up at him with hands-on-hips.

Trouble.

Despite his limited English, Dino recognized the word. His chest tightened with apprehension. But pot-bellied, silver-whiskered Mr. Phillips had spoken it while chuckling. Things couldn't have been all bad.

"Emily keeps telling her friends that Jesse Katsopoulos from *Full House* is painting her home. We'll be surrounded by screaming teeny-boppers in a minute here!"

"Ah, yes…..I see."

Mr. Phillips chuckled again, his belly bobbing. "You haven't the slightest idea what I mean, huh? You got a lot to learn about the U-S-of-A, my boy. And not just pop culture. That's why I'm having you paint my house before we send you off to real customers. You make a mistake here, hell, I don't mind. Someone shelling out cash might have a different view, however. Come down and let me show you something."

Dino stood a head or two taller than his boss after descending the ladder. Still, he felt as if the man towered over him. Mr. Phillips's voice might have been friendly, though his gaze was stern. Those eyes, golden like a fox's, were punctuated at the outer corners by tiny lines etched as if time had marked its claim via blade. While clouds shifted and shadows befell them, Dino recalled stories his father, Konstantine, had told of a childhood spent laboring beneath such stares. Neither the Mediterranean heat, nor the job's physical demands had worn him down. What did him in, was the omnipotent scrutiny of his foreman.

"Now look here," Mr. Phillips said, taking hold of Dino's hand. "Your technique might do fine back in the old country where people seem to take their sweet time, but I want to see you doing things more like this . . ." Dino watched as Mr. Phillips manipulated his wrist in a fluid, sweeping motion that felt akin to what Dino had already been doing. "See that there?" Mr. Phillips started up again, "Controlled, precise, quick. Aw, don't look at me like that, son. I'm not saying your method is wrong. This one is just *better*, see?"

Dino stayed quiet and re-climbed the ladder.

"Now that's it," said Mr. Phillips, "almost. You just need a bit more . . . hmm . . . *flick* in your wrist, I guess."

Dino took a deep breath, and then went on adding color to the faded wood. At one point he heard a scraping through the gravel below, and saw Mr. Phillips setting up another ladder. Dino tried to focus on the work, but then his boss appeared next to him on a top rung. Mr. Phillips didn't say anything, though from the corner of his vision Dino watched the man watching him; those fox eyes slanted to amber dashes. Sweat beaded Dino's forehead.

"Don't forget to smooth out those drips," said Mr. Phillips.

Dino moved his wrist up and down, listened to the tiny clicks of his joints.

"Now that's not quite how I showed you," Mr. Phillips chimed in again. "But you're getting there."

Dino felt a throbbing in his temples, the sun directly above his head now.

"See," The boss's voice blotted Dino's concentration a third time, "You're making more work for yourself if you try and fill in the gaps on a first coat."

Dino clenched his teeth. Still, he went on painting, trying to sync his form with the older man's vague pointers.

"Daddy! Can you guys take a break for a minute so Tiffany can meet Mr. Kouros?"

Emily Phillips and her friend Tiffany, brace-faced preteens with flowing yellow hair, stood between the two ladders and stared up at Dino with an eager desire that made him blush. He exchanged a glance with his boss.

"I suppose we're due for a break here, huh?" said Mr. Phillips.

Blushing with hands behind his back while the girls yammered like village goats, Dino sat at a table in the garden. Amid bursts of orange nasturtiums, he sipped from a glass of lemonade as Mr. Phillips batted his big straw hat to provoke a breeze. The man had been sitting across from him, so quiet that Dino worried real trouble had reared its head. But then Mr. Phillips said, "You've done great today, son. I know it's hot, and I been pestering you about silly details. But that's just because I was testing you, see? You're bound to get nitpicking customers. Always keep your cool."

In solitary moments, Alex Kouros wondered if, like eye color, some memories were hereditary traits passed from one generation to the next—a tendency toward nostalgia, perhaps, or a predisposed diversion to particular kinds of work. He had heard of *collective memory*—recollections shared among a group—but understood that to mean two or more people thinking back on occurrences in which they'd both taken part. Had he been wiser, a little more book-smart, he might've known a word for when you so vividly remembered the details of an event, despite never having experienced it. His father Dino's first day on the job after arriving from Greece was one of those events. Alex hadn't yet been conceived. Or, at the very least, he had still been in the womb. But so often had he heard the story, he had trouble deciphering whether the memory belonged to him or his father.

The last time Alex had held a "real" job he was nineteen. Mom seemed fine with her son getting by via internet Poker bets and moonlighting haircuts at the occasional barbershop. But Dad wanted him to have the respectable experience of being an employee. Alex told himself that an impatience to leave the teen years behind had propelled him out into the big, bad world of IRA-amassing grown-ups. He took a gig at a bland corporate office, and spent those blandest of hours between nine and five sitting in front of a computer entering even blander data.

While dozing through night classes in effort to complete his degree in Business Management, he had taken the grossly mis-titled position of "Data Processing Specialist," or DPS. Dino had, once again, told of that day on the ladder when Mr. Phillips bestowed an important lesson.

"You learn the value of patience," Dino had said. "Someone get on you, keep you in line, and you don't lose your cold."

"Your *cool*, Dad. Don't lose your cool."

"Well, whatever. Just keep cold, and maybe, like me, you one day be your own boss. I got better little by little, until I was even a little better than Mister Phillips. The American dream, yes? Be better until you the best."

Alex and his father's differing point-of-views were most apparent on a particular day at his last place of official employment. As a means of shaking rust from his hustler stride, he handed out fliers for his latest party promotion. Along with ensuring the venue filled to capacity, he hoped his colleagues might repay his generosity by helping him succeed in the office.

A few of the higher up's—James, VP of Marketing; Tina, supervisor to Alex's supervisor—awarded him high-fives as he slipped them the advertisement. With renewed vigor, Alex strode to his tiny cubicle. Corporate couldn't knock the hustle.

"Alex."

He should have known not to let his optimism soar too high. The voice summoned him back to earth. Gina. A square-jawed woman at least twenty years his senior, sporting a bobbed haircut, she had always reminded Alex of a boarding school principal; the type who would threaten boys with a ruler, then order them into her office to spank her using the same yardstick.

"You might consider organizing those files by priority to allow for faster input."

Out of the corner of his eye, Alex scanned the paper stack. "It's okay. I prefer to input the lengthier reports first."

"That's generally the best strategy, but today the shorter abstracts are a higher priority."

Alex cleared his throat. "I saw that on the board, and actually have them done already." Keeping his eyes on the monitor, he felt the woman leaning in to examine his desk.

"If that's so, you should shred the copies. Remember, confidentiality is key when dealing with such info."

"Thanks. I'll get to that right away."

"Yes, make sure you do. Just because you're a top Tech doesn't mean I don't have my eye on you."

"Understood, ma'am." Alex, ready to get back on task, had to lean aside for a moment as the supervisor conducted an over-the-shoulder inspection of his computer screen.

"Keep your eyes peeled at all times," Gina said. "Top row, center. That should be an 'E', not a 'B'."

"Thanks. I'm on it." When the woman turned to go, Alex thought he could get back on track. But then:

"Oh, and watch your tie-knot next time."

Alex felt his cheeks redden.

"Relax, I'm only kidding."

While refilling his coffee mug in the break room, Alex felt a touch between his shoulder blades. He turned to find the supervisor rubbing his back, and she left her hand there for a moment after he'd noticed.

"Thanks for getting those files in ahead of deadline. I can always count on you. Not often we hire somebody with a work ethic as good as their good looks."

Alex took a step back, hoping to conceal his red cheeks behind the rim of the cup as he went for a sip. "No problem, Ms. Watters."

"Please. I've told you before, call me Gina. We've been working together for, what, almost four months now? I practically see you as one of my friends at this point."

"Nice." The only reply Alex could muster while stepping aside to give Gina free reign of the sink. In moving past him, she brushed her palm along his back again, lower this time. Alex made for the door as fast as he could without breaking into a full jog.

"Alex, wait."

He clenched his teeth before a curse could escape his lips. "Yes?"

"I can't help noticing you've never joined us for the company happy hours. Your presence has been missed."

"Why? Am I expected to take care of the first round?" Alex asked with a chuckle. "I'm sure everyone's gotten by just fine."

Gina's smile gleamed fuschia like gloss painted on a shark's grin. "Do try and make it sometime."

Alex offered a polite nod, then spun on his heel to finally make an escape.

"One more thing. Can't help noticing you fixed your tie."

"Like you always say, 'it's all in the details,' right?"

Gina laughed harder than necessary. "Here, let me help."

"Really, it's—"

Gina's hands were at this throat before he could protest. "That's a great color on you, by the way," she said while running her fingertip along the length of his orange tie. "Brings out your Mediterranean complexion."

"What can I say? I'm all Greek."

"You certainly are. Take it easy the rest of the day, Alex. You've earned some fluff tasks."

Of course Alex dealt with douchebags while cutting hair, or flipping phones, or any number of side hustles he perpetuated on his own time. Clients played games, occasionally tried to get over on him, but no comparison to what he witnessed in the corporate world. Despite being relatively low in rank, coworkers tried to trample him at every ladder step on their way to the elusive and mysterious "top." He had always assumed the stereotypical nine-to-five only existed on TV. Here he was, however, in a sitcom-worthy saga of the lowest ratings.

He should've known better than to take to heart the granted permission to engage in "fluff activities." But in a moment of bad judgment he logged onto his personal Facebook account following an update of the company profile.

"Alex!"

He turned and froze upon finding James behind him. But then the guy added, "Careful, bro! We got a mouse in our cheese!"

Alex heeded James's warning and logged off social media, only to be summoned to Ms. Watters's office anyhow.

"I got word you wanted to see me?"

Gina sat with hands clasped in front of her, lips pursed to a perfect single line. "Take a seat please." In her voice no trace of the chummy tone from an hour or so earlier when she'd inquired about Alex's weekend plans. "You know, Alex, when I first got hired at this company, my boss was Mr. Donaldson, though everyone called him Young Santa Claus. But even more than his appearance, his personality fit the nickname to a 'T.' We were his 'elves,' happy to keep the 'workshop' running."

"You see," Gina continued, her tongue darting out to trace the fuschia contour of her upper lip, "every Friday morning, to reward us for the week's hard work, Mr. Donaldson brought donuts. He'd set them in the break room, take a raspberry jelly, then leave us to enjoy the rest. There were enough so each of us got one, and trust me, one was plenty as these were the biggest, most decadent donuts I'd ever seen. But as this Friday tradition carried on, someone started taking it for granted."

Gina paused again, unclasping and re-clasping her hands. Alex sat a little straighter in the chair, clasped his hands, too.

"Now just like Santa, our boss eventually found out who had been naughty instead of nice, and he came down real hard on the culprit. Took him into the office and read him the riot act. The following Friday there were no donuts."

Gina sat back in her chair and spread her cocktail wiener-shaped fingers, nails polished ketchup red, across the desktop. "You've heard the story, Alex, now from you I'd like to hear the lesson."

"I don't suppose you're going to offer me a donut?"

Gina flashed the ghost of a smile. "I try to be a friend, Alex. But it seems you've taken that friendship for granted. It's come to my attention that you've been surfing Facebook on company time?"

"I'm sorry for the mistake," said Alex. "No excuses."

"I've discussed protocol as it pertains to using the Web, Alex. Earlier, when I mentioned you could engage in 'fluff activities' between projects, I meant something like taking a stretch and tidying up your workspace."

Gina's lips moved, but Alex missed the diatribe, listening instead to his father's footsteps on the ladder. He visualized the man standing on the top rung. Alex rose from the chair and undid his tie. "Thanks for teaching me I need to be my own boss." He felt the woman's eyes on him as he turned to leave. He didn't look back.

Later, coming down off the adrenaline rush that had accompanied telling his supervisor to, basically, choke on all her sweet treat analogies, at the kitchen table Alex struggled to focus on the current chapter in his Business Management book.

"Hey, how come you not at work?" Dino Kouros entered the kitchen in coveralls so paint-stained that Alex wondered if the man, owner of a house painting company now, could afford to get more pigment on his clothes than he did on walls.

"Quit my job at the office."

Dino grabbed a chair and collapsed into it. "Quit? Why?"

"It wasn't for me, Dad." Alex figured his father wouldn't understand.

"What do you mean it 'wasn't for you,' re?" Dino asked. "Work is for everybody. When I was painting for Mr. Phillips, he always said—"

"Dad, please," Alex cut in. From his coat pocket he withdrew his orange necktie and held it out to Dino like that most clichéd of Fathers Day gifts. "When I first started at the office I could barely get the knot right. Then, it seemed I got the hang of it. But I finally realized I wasn't tying a better knot, just a tighter one. Each day tighter than the day before, until I could hardly breathe. There's no ladder to climb at the office job, at least not one leading to any place I want to go."

Dino stood up from the couch and contemplated his coveralls as if his thoughts were mapped across those paint blots. "When you were a boy I always spoke to you of Greece; the sea and sun. But now I wonder if maybe I should have tried to raise you with more . . . what is the word? . . . *sensibilities* of Americans. People here know that making a living is the top priority. Maybe that was lost on you."

"Of course I want to make a good living, Dad."

"With what?"

"Art," Alex said.

Dino made a face. "But you're not an artist."

Alex's shoulders sank. "The city's changing. Oakland is becoming an artist's town again. I want to be involved somehow, to be at the center of the movement. Money will come."

Dino lowered his eyes, fingered his jaw and seemed to consider. "Perhaps you will open your own gallery. There is power in running a business. Now, in the meantime, why not work with me for a while?"

"I've never been great with heights."

"Fine. I guess you have the Poker to hold you over for now. That seems fine by your mother at least."

"That, the haircutting, and my True Town Tours gig . . ."

"A man of many trades is a man of none."

"Not sure that's a real saying, Dad, but I feel you."

One evening in December before his twenty-sixth birthday, Alex stood on the stage of a downtown Oakland venue watching a man atop a ladder as he hung a banner reading TOWN BIZ ART FESTIVAL.

"How's that look, Mr. Kouros?"

Alex stepped back to contemplate the sign shimmering green-and-gold, A's colors, beneath the glow of theater lights, and back-dropped by curtains of wine-colored velour. He beamed over a job well done. Months of planning and orchestrating had culminated with the raising of that sign, the fest only a day away now. A showcase of talented locals, be they musicians, poets, or painters, the event felt like the fulfillment of a dream belonging to both he and his father—a collective ambition. "No need to call me 'mister,' my friend."

The worker raised his eyebrows and peered down at Alex.

Alex chuckled. "'Alex' is fine."

"Okay, Alex. You want, I can move it a little more to the center."

"No, Hector, it's okay. Why not take a break."

Hector shrugged and descended the ladder. Alex waited until he was alone, then stood center-stage gazing out at the all seats reminiscent of those ancient amphitheaters in Greece as he imagined the audience gathered in anticipation of those poets, musicians, and dancers soon to grace the platform.

we grew here

Near evening, they returned to the village. Treetop doves cooed their anticipation of the looming twilight. Angelo Koutouvalis awakened from a beach-day induced nap as the truck pulled up to a modest, two-story ocean-front house of white stucco. Beyond its wrought-iron entry gate a lush garden blossomed with striped petunias, red hibiscus, and, most abundantly, pink shocks of bougainvillea. Angelo's paternal grandmother, *yiayia* Eleni, occupied the home's lower level while Aunt Voula and Uncle Elias resided up top.

Aunt Voula, a guitar-shaped woman with an easy smile, hugged Angelo as he stepped onto the veranda. "Welcome home! Just in time to eat after your day in the sea!"

"I'm definitely hungry, *Thea*."

The family gathered at the kitchen table for a meal of rooster braised in tomato sauce served over spaghetti.

Arms resting atop the round of his impressive belly, Uncle Elias announced, "On the way over, Angelo was telling me that, unlike him, his American friends do not live in the family home. Many Americans only see their uncles and aunts on Christmas."

Voula raised an eyebrow. "Is that so?"

"For the most part," Angelo said.

Voula sipped wine. "It seems Americans are closer to their dogs than to their grown children."

Uncle Elias chuckled. Among Angelo's extended family, laughter proved contagious.

They spent the warm evening—vocal with the lulling drone of crickets—out on the balcony, watching the ebb and flow of the sea, its waves undulating a dark, sensuous dance against the shoreline. There, beneath the moon, among the company of his father, aunt, and uncle, Angelo felt at home. No matter that his true home awaited an ocean away.

The next morning, Angelo and Uncle Elias strolled down to the harbor. The village was empty besides a scattering of silver-haired men seated outside the *kafenions* perusing newspapers and sipping *kafe*. Along the dock, a dozen or so fishing and sailboats. The majority of them flew the Greek flag, its blue-and-white stripes casting a noble sight against the rapidly brightening sky.

"That is my boat there," said Uncle Elias, indicating a modest vessel. The name 'ARTEMIS' was scripted across its flank. "I need you to come fishing with me because my partner Pavlos is in Athens on business for the next couple days. You haven't forgotten how to fish since your last visit so many years ago?"

"Of course not." Angelo took a deep breath and straddled one foot on the dock, the other on the boat. He managed to climb aboard without landing in the water. Elias boarded effortlessly, and Angelo, at his uncle's command, sat near the bow while the motor cranked. Once they reached the desired depths, Elias killed the engine before enlisting Angelo's help in casting the nets. Finally, he sat back to enjoy a cigarette while Angelo sipped from a bottled water.

"This image on your T-shirt," began Elias, "reminds me of an American movie I've seen, though I don't recall the name."

Alex pulled at the bottom of his Tee and looked down at the graphic gracing its front: The hand of a puppeteer holding strings from which hung the phrase *The Bay Area*. "You're thinking of *The Godfather*. This is a play off of that, but it's just about representing where I'm from. Oakland, y'know?"

"Tell me more about things in Oakland. We worry for you when we see news reports from the large American cities. They are often dangerous, no?"

Angelo felt his blood roaring in his ears. On the distant horizon he spotted a greenish landmass. The island of Spetses or Hydra? No matter, Oakland seemed *worlds* away now. "It's not so bad where I live, Uncle. The city is changing, for better *and* worse. Rich people are moving in, and driving the poorer people out. Many new businesses are opening. It's a good place to be an artist right now. There's this feeling that you can be part of something big. I guess I'm trying to find where I fit in the whole scene. Oakland has always been a city of go-getters, and we support our home-grown talent."

Elias seemed to consider. "Family helping family."

Angelo nodded. "And family is everything here."

"Yes, it is."

They sat in silence for a time, Angelo watching the dappled sunlight play off the waves in web-like patterns. When it came time to check the nets, he helped his uncle pull them in, muscles straining with the effort, the rough rope biting into his palms.

"*Bravo!*" Elias exclaimed once the catch had been lifted aboard.

The nets were full of reddish-pink fish, and Angelo watched their tiny mouths gape.

Angelo found a figure at his bedside. He'd just opened his eyes, stirred from a dream of flight; ironic given these tugs of jet-lag that made any ascent into dreamland difficult. His back to the window, he blinked to be certain he wasn't still asleep. The shadowy visitor, undoubtedly real, also remained motionless. This vague human form, stooped like a hunchback, held something in its hand. In the moonbeam, the object glinted bright and metallic. At the depths of his chest, Angelo's breath clung like ice. He counted the seconds. One . . . two. At three he fired his hand toward the nightstand, clicked on the lamp. Alex blinked again. The new brightness revealed Yiayia standing in place of his potential killer, the thing cradled in her withered grasp a shiny picture frame rather than a polished weapon. "Yiayia," Angelo said, "what are you doing?"

"Father?" the woman asked.

Angelo sat up. Yiayia held a sepia-tone portrait of her parents, Angelo's great-grandparents, who had died long before he'd been born. Konstantine, Angelo's *Proto-Papou*, whom Yiayia indicated with her finger, boasted massive shoulders and an oiled mustache curled at the edges—resembling something between a carnival strongman and the Greek rural farmer he'd been.

"Where is Father?" Yiayia said again.

Angelo put a gentle hand on Yiayia's delicate forearm. Her big-eyed gaze seemed almost childlike. Since his recent return after those five weeks in Greece, Angelo thought Yiayia's hair shone with a deeper shade of silver; the lines etched across her face holding a new ferocity.

"Take me to Father. I need to see him!"

Angelo shivered at Yiayia's request. Still, he didn't have the heart to remind her of the wish's impossibility. When he rose from bed, slowly as to not startle the elderly woman, she staggered backward anyhow. The sight left a slash deep in Angelo's chest.

"It's me, Yiayia. It's Angelo. Let's get you back to bed." He escorted her to the room across the hall and tucked her beneath her bed covers.

The next morning, in his room Angelo sat contemplating the manuscript of his graphic novel titled *Harpoons* and featuring the adventures of his suave Mediterranean hero. The pages of illustrations were stacked over a hundred sheets thick. He'd be done with the draft by the conclusion of grad school next Spring, but who, beyond his art professors and his family, would care?

In the kitchen, Angelo greeted his mother sitting at the counter sipping her coffee.

"What are your plans for this Saturday?"

"It's summer, Ma," Angelo said, pouring cereal. "Every day feels like Saturday."

"Don't I know. In a few weeks I'll be back to grading student papers again."

"And I'll be suffering through critiques."

"Not that bad, is it?"

Angelo regarded the yard-facing window, waiting for birds that failed to appear. "I'm heading out soon, but I'll leave the money on the dining room table."

"Money for what, hon'?"

Angelo downed the remainder of his Raisin Bran, though he no longer felt hungry. Turning away from his mother, he washed the bowl in the sink. "I arrived home on the fifteenth and forgot to pay you. It's now the thirtieth."

"Why don't you just pay me on the first?"

To Angelo's ears, the water moving through the pipes whooshed like air in a plane's cabin. "Because then I'd be putting money toward September's rent."

Despina sighed. "This is getting complicated, Angelo. I told you not to worry about—"

"The cousins back in the *horyo* all live at home still."

"And most are in their twenties, just like you. So, what's the big deal?"

Angelo felt pressure building in his chest. "It's not . . . forget it, okay?"

"You brought it up."

"I know, Ma. Sorry." Angelo kissed his mother on the cheek and headed for the front door, passing Yiayia's room. She was in bed. He still hadn't gotten used to the fact that she no longer protested when he left the house.

Angelo sauntered down the block, parallel tree branches clasped like the fingers of worried hands, and recalled his mother informing him, just before the end of his Greece journey, that Yiayia had succumbed to the early stages of Dementia. Yiayia was growing forgetful, but she still recognized family. Angelo had tried to prepare, though he now realized he hadn't prepared well enough.

He sat on a bench outside the train station, turning away at the sight of an elderly couple pushing a girl in a stroller. When they paused near his resting spot to check on the toddler, Angelo got up and headed for the BART platform. He boarded a train and disembarked at the wrong downtown stop—12th St. instead of 19th—due to meet Phaedra in twenty minutes for lunch at Rudy's over on Telegraph.

He moved to the opposite sidewalk, ambling through a haze of fatigue, and bought an energy drink from De Lauer's after briefly, and unsuccessfully, skimming the international news racks for a Greek paper. Back outside, chatter swirling around him, Angelo still half-expected to hear the mother tongue spoken amid the breeze. Noon in California meant it was ten at night in Greece. Hardly late by Mediterranean standards, but Angelo felt as though half his brain still slumbered back in the village.

A car horn broke the trance. Angelo again found himself amid pedestrian traffic on an Oakland street not so suited for standing with eyes shut, even on a bright, Saturday afternoon. Phaedra strolled up at twelve-thirty sharp; her tall stride, that storm of dark curls flowing past her shoulders, those eyes the color of beach stones all resonating with the same newness with which everything had been bestowed once Angelo stepped off his return flight. Her beauty was the only thing retaining the glow in recent days, however. No one could believe he'd met this girl on a plane.

Through Angelo's window view, the jetliner's wing seemed to reach across the runway's full expanse, only an arc of the gloomy sky visible beyond.

"I guess this is me," a young woman said, stowing her luggage overhead before taking the seat next to him. "I'm Phaedra, by the way."

Angelo smiled. "Angelo."

"Hey, buddy, you still with me over there?"

Angelo blinked. Phaedra waved at him from across their table at Rudy's. Its clear plastic surface gave view of the trinkets molded within: pocket knives, kid-sized scissors, nail files. "Ah, sorry. Didn't get much sleep last night."

Phaedra smiled. "No worries. Just looked like you were somewhere far, far away."

"Missing Greece, I guess."

"Paradise? You're not the only one."

"The beauty's one thing, but going back after so many years, seeing my dad, it reminded me how close families are over there. I was still in high school when Dad left after my folks split. It was just Mom and I then, and Dad was this missing piece across the ocean; larger-than-life and out of reach."

"But you've bridged the gap," Phaedra said. "Bravo. What do you mean by larger-than-life?"

"He's cool, a real *mangka*, y' know? And really good-looking..."

Phaedra smiled. "As are you."

Angelo felt his cheeks darken, and Phaedra laughed.

"So," she said, "he's 'The Most Interesting Man in the Universe, basically?"

"Pretty much."

Angelo's stomach dipped as it had when the plane began its descent over San Francisco. Now, in seeking something solid, something firmly entrenched to the ground, he studied the table again. No telling what the trinket display meant, though the sight of sharp objects safely contained seemed vaguely reassuring.

"For what it's worth," Phaedra said, "I think it's pretty cool you have that closeness with your mom and *yiayia*. You get to save money and focus on your art. It's a luxury most can't afford in this country."

Angelo nodded. "In Greece, I stayed at my *yiayia's* house with my aunt and uncle upstairs. Every evening, other relatives would visit ... more aunts and uncles, cousins ... and we'd all sit out in the yard under the citrus trees and just be *together*."

"I'm lucky that most of my relatives are here," Phaedra said. "They all moved over from the old country together and they stayed together, just like you say."

"So, you don't think it's weird? Me still living at home as a twenty-four-year-old."

"Like I said," Phaedra began, "I envy your situation as it allows you to focus on your art. My only concern is that if your living situation changes . . . for whatever reason . . . will you be able to support yourself?"

Angelo felt heat at his cheeks. "Why wouldn't I be? I'll get another day job when I need one."

Phaedra smiled. "That easy? Ah, to be a man in the workforce. If I could write my stories full time, I would. But, Greek family or not, I don't have that luxury. By twenty, I was out of the house and I didn't want to ask for help. So, paralegal work it is."

Angelo resisted the temptation to sigh as he went for a menu. Phaedra was an artist in her own right, though from what Angelo had witnessed in the couple weeks they had been dating, she treated her craft as a hobby in between her paralegal gig.

"Angelo, I mean it when I say you're lucky. Chase your dream. Hell, I'd love to live with my folks. But I know we'd eventually kill each other."

"That's a shame."

Phaedra shrugged. "You're Greek. Our families, close and all, are pretty intense."

"In Greece, and other countries, it seems, they value art more than we do."

Phaedra glanced up from her menu. "Do you know Alex Kouros?"

Angelo shook his head.

"He's not an artist, at least not in the traditional sense, but the guy's heavy in the scene. Seems like a good person to have on your side."

"But we've got the same initials."

"So?"

"People might get us confused. Two Greeks making the local rounds, both with first names that begin with 'A' and last names starting with 'K?'"

Phaedra chuckled. "You worry about the strangest things."

Angelo shrugged. "Just be glad you didn't meet me *before* the latest trip to Greece. I was an anxious wreck afraid to fly. That's why I stayed away so long from the fatherland."

After lunch, they turned the corner and strolled hand-in-hand past the Fox Theater. Across the street the old Sears building stood boarded up and abandoned like a neglected grandparent to the block's newer establishments. Angelo recalled a few years prior, the last time he'd been inside the still operating department store, when he'd accompanied Yiayia on a trip to select a new washing machine. The clerk had commented on Angelo's good nature in helping his grandmother run her errand. He'd smiled shyly, and Yiayia, beaming, had proclaimed, "Yes, he is a sweet boy. The light of my life."

Angelo regarded Phaedra with a smile and tightened his grip on her hand. They headed this way because she wanted to show him a recent exhibit in a small, newish gallery a couple blocks up. Supposedly the artist's style reminded her of his. She claimed seeing this painter's work would remind Angelo that he, too, could make a living with his art. Angelo, however, remained skeptical.

When they arrived at the gallery, it appeared as welcoming as the shell of the Sears building; the windows vacant save for a big FOR LEASE sign. Alex exchanged glances with Phaedra, though she looked equally perplexed.

"This place had only been here a year, and despite it being off the main drag, as far as galleries go, it seemed to do well. I came by just last week. The exhibit I'd told you about was still up and everything."

Angelo shrugged again. "Maybe it was a little *too* far off the main drag after all."

"Hey! Fuck you, bro!"

Angelo followed Phaedra's gaze to the end of the block where a small crowd hoisting signs reading "OAKLAND: WE GREW HERE, YOU FLEW HERE!" and "TAKE A HIKE! NO MORE RENT SPIKES!" confronted a comparable crowd of mostly white twenty-somethings in flannel shirts, Doc Martens, and lens-less glasses. Upon closer look, the protesters also wore shirts that said, "SAVE YOUR NEIGHBORHOOD! KILL A HIPSTER!" On either side of the argument, the participants, with their cartoonish scowls and angry exclamations held above their heads like word bubbles, reminded Angelo of something he might find in a comic book. Perhaps the scene would even work its way into his graphic novel.

Apart from the hurled obscenities, the dynamic seemed relatively peaceful; neither group fully infringed on one other's space as though a line had been chalked along the pavement. Still, a trio of hulking bicycle cops pedaled to the edge of the commotion.

When Phaedra suggested they investigate, Angelo felt his stomach knot. But, wanting to appear brave in front of his date, he led her toward the fuss. To Angelo's surprise, among the culturally-mixed ten to fifteen protesters, there were at least a handful of elderly people—not quite as old as Yiayia, but gray nonetheless—gruff old radical types braving the generation gap in the name of what they believed was right.

"...Not our fault we came from someplace else!" Proclaimed a man bearded like a lumberjack despite the likelihood, given his two-by-four physique, that he'd never once chopped wood. "We're just trying to make a home for ourselves and you people treat us like we're part of a corporate plot!"

"What you mean you *people?*" asked a black guy around Angelo's age. The historically familiar question inspired a few chuckles amid the protestors, though of course none of the gentrifiers dared laugh. The black man shoved the faux lumberjack, triggering a collective gasp through the crowd. Then, with an almost theatrical backstep, the opposing sides simultaneously retreated as though following a script. "You wanna talk about home?" asked a silver-haired Latina as she muscled her way to the front of the pack despite her own delicate frame. "For years I lived above that shop," she said, vaguely gesturing toward the vacant gallery, "but I can't afford it anymore, so I live with my daughter and grandchildren!"

"Hey, lady, I'm sorry, but *I* didn't personally run up your rent!" shouted another hipster.

"You want to make a home here?" Asked someone on the local side of the line, "Try acknowledging your neighbors when you see us on the street instead of holding your smug heads high!"

"Yeah, that slogan on your shirt is real neighborly alright!"

With that comment the air between the two groups seemed to shift, the opposing forces physically butting up against each other again, a few people even standing chest to chest. Despite her prior curiosity, Phaedra backpedaled a few paces, Angelo secretly glad for the new vantage point. But then the cops stepped in, commanding everyone to disperse. After a few grumbles, and another round of traded insults, the crowds broke off in opposite directions.

"You're an Oakland native. How'd all that make you feel?" Phaedra asked in the aftermath.

"I guess 'home' isn't a word to be taken lightly these days. Maybe I really should feel more fortunate I've got a house I'm due to inherit someday, despite having to share it with family now."

"And family's not a bad word."

Angelo gazed into the horizon. "Not at all."

They cut back over to 19th and Broadway, train station bound, Angelo unable to help doing a double-take every time he saw a man or woman sporting skinny jeans, tattered Chucks, and old Zac Efron-haircut as though the combination marked them as rival gang members on the wrong turf. If transplants—at least the type who hoped to make the city over as some white-washed, artisan utopia—didn't want trouble, why did they wear clothes that left them so conspicuous? They were suddenly to blame for his inability to afford rent in the city in which he'd been raised, no matter if he chose to grind it out as an artist or land a day job in the corporate world. They were the reason he had to share the family home.

As if mirroring Angelo's thoughts, Phaedra remarked, "When my parents arrived from Greece they, like most immigrants before them, joined the larger community without diluting it. I don't get why these people can't do the same."

"Sounds like at your paralegal job you take on lots of complaints from locals," Angelo said.

"Totally," Phaedra replied. "Filing harassment reports is an everyday grind. Last week, we received one from a long-time resident over West, sweet old gentleman who's been in the neighborhood for, I don't know, forty, fifty years? He says the new couple next door threatens to call the cops whenever he's out after dark walking his dog. Each time, they say he looks 'suspicious,' like they've never seen him before."

Angelo sighed. "A variation of 'all black people look alike,' huh?"

"Unfortunately."

Angelo and Phaedra caught their train, but heading home wasn't an option. Angelo didn't sense this was an ideal time to introduce Phaedra to his mother and grandmother. Phaedra, meanwhile, lived clear out in

Walnut Creek. Angelo didn't feel like taking BART all the way out there and back, regardless as to whether or not Phaedra offered to let him stay the night. In the end, Angelo felt water beckon to him, and they decided to spend the remainder of the afternoon at the Lake.

"In Greece it's not just that generations of families tend to live together, at least in the *horyo*," Angelo said while, from his spot in the grass next to Phaedra, pondering a pair of paddle boats drifting amid the looming twilight. "They do it because they want to, not because rents are too high and the kids have nowhere else to go."

"So, that's how you feel?" Phaedra asked after taking a sip of sparkling lemonade from one of the cans they'd purchased at a corner market. "You've got no other options?"

Now Angelo watched pigeons flutter from tree to tree, just as his thoughts failed to find a suitable nesting place. "Maybe," he said. "At least the gentrifiers had that choice, you know? Instead of staying with their families, they decided to colonize the Oakland frontier. Right or wrong, they've got conviction. I'll give them that much credit."

Phaedra chuckled. "You don't strike me as the colonizing type."

"I didn't say I'm on their side, I just recognize their guts."

"I think the locals have guts to stand up to them."

Angelo shrugged. "Both sides looked funny out there, marching around with their chests puffed like superheroes."

"Maybe it takes looking funny to get a point across."

Angelo turned toward Phaedra and put a hand to his brow in an effort to discern her face against the setting sun's rosy blush. "You might be right."

To the left of their towel, some twenty yards across the grass, a quartet of shirtless black teens were scolded by roving police for playing a boombox too loud. Angelo had barely noticed the music until the cops brought it to attention. He watched the youths try to argue, then finally gather their things and stomp off in a huff; four dark silhouettes in the waning dusk.

"We should do something..." Phaedra said.

"Like what?" Angelo asked with a helpless spread of his palms. "The cops know what side they're on, and it sure isn't ours."

Angelo and Phaedra made the evening news. Technically, at least. For an instant there they were as the camera panned out to showcase a wide view of the downtown protest, the two of them standing on the fringe.

On TV, the "Oakland rally against gentrification," as the reporter coined it, looked more like a schoolyard confrontation. Despite the large screen, both the hipsters and the locals appeared small and cartoonish with their overly dramatic gestures and huff-and-puff proclamations; Angelo again reminded of comic book heroes thumping their chests amid illustration panels.

The cameras caught him and Phaedra in profile, though neither his mother nor Yiayia seemed to notice. Despina sat in her chair paging through a magazine in between glances over at Yiayia, who, in shuffling slippers, kept edging toward the front door as if plotting another escape.

"Mother, come sit down!"

Yiayia, head hanging in defeat, reluctantly obeyed.

Angelo couldn't help smiling at himself, no matter how brief his cameo. The news crew must have conducted their interviews after the cops broke up the rally and he and Phaedra left the scene. Angelo didn't recall seeing any reporters around. Nevertheless, there stood a correspondent with a microphone poised like an ice cream cone beneath the chin of a man obviously sporting a SAVE YOUR NEIGHBORHOOD! KILL

A HIPSTER! T-shirt, despite the fact that the word "kill" had now been blurred out. That seemed strange. Were tensions really so thick that the media feared someone might actually carry out the wearable command?

The protestor said something about home; Oakland no longer feeling like *home*, locals being forced out of their homes, new homes crowding out old homes. Angelo stopped listening to the specifics, again ruminating on that one word. He was **home** again, Yiayia was *home* again.

His mother had been shocked to see them walk through the door; Angelo holding his grandmother's arm, Yiayia neglecting to relinquish the sketch pad.

Apparently, Despina had been at the stove making *avgalemono* soup when Yiayia slipped out the first time. A five or so minute lapse of Despina's attention was all Yiayia had needed to grab the sketchpad and head out the door.

"Well, that's really a shame, isn't it?" asked Despina now.

The news imagery depicted an organ in distress; the heart of down-town Oakland's arts district simply a row of shut doors and dark windows accompanying the newscaster's hollow voiceover tale of rising rent and drained funds.

Despina, eyes still on the screen, said, "Too bad you didn't finish your graphic novel sooner, hon."

Angelo frowned. "What do you mean?"

"Oh," Despina began, "I just meant that with timing on your side, you might have found a real home in the local art scene. It's a shame how things don't always work out."

He lay on his bed, head propped on the pillow, half the manuscript piled on his bare chest as he skimmed through pages at random. The Greek, *Super Kamaki*, a cross between a Mediterranean James Bond and the long lost thirteenth deity in the Olympian pantheon: swarthy gent wearing a knowing smirk while leaving footprints of lightning in his wake.

As he sprawled on his comforter now, Angelo wondered if he still had time to thread the theme of gentrification into the work, have The Greek battle Big Business and clueless transplants alike as they attempted to decimate his beloved Greektown with yoga studios and gluten-free bakeries. He went so far as to snag a blank sheet and sketch his wavy-haired hero standing up to a horde of Pabst-swilling perpetrators.

He heard muffled voices down the hall; Yiayia and Despina speaking above the TV's din. Yiayia rarely spoke at length, though she apparently had a lot to say tonight. The sound filled Angelo with a certain warmth. He recalled that in Greek mythology the goddess Hestia is ruler of the hearth, the fireplace, the home.

A Google search was everything. Angelo typed Alex's name and the Internet gushed its enthusiasm. Many links to choose from, his first click led to an image of Alex Kouros on stage downtown at The Golden Bull, that divey venue of "True Town" aesthetics. In the photo, Alex leaned into a microphone while holding a sheet of paper inches from his roaring mouth. Angelo had never been a huge fan of Slam Poetry with all its histrionics, but he admitted Alex looked the part of charismatic griot.

Angelo chose one last link and found himself at Alex's personal website, a rather professional-looking page featuring a chiseled-cheek-bone-highlighting-headshot presiding over a brief bio leading into the site's main purpose: the advertising of Alex's TRUE TOWN TOURS. Angelo immediately wanted to get Alex's perspective on this issue of "home" as it pertained to the city's changing dynamics. He wondered what Alex thought of today's protest news coverage, eager to hear the guy's opinion on the SAVE YOUR NEIGHBORHOOD T-shirts, and the overall state of the art scene given that Alex seemed to thoroughly operate on its fringes.

Angelo called Phaedra. "Babe, can you arrange a meeting with Alex?"

"Now? What's the rush?"

"Like Mom says, gotta strike while the timing is right."

"I'll give him a call."

As if a rendezvous with Alexander the Great had already been confirmed, Angelo strode with pride into his bedroom just as the phone rang.

"Babe!"

"Hey, you. Great news! Alex says your graphic novel has a 'really cool concept,' and he wants to see an excerpt during tomorrow's meet up."

"That's awesome! With all his connections, maybe he knows a guy who knows a guy, you know?"

"I do. Now, why don't you come stay at my place tonight?"

"Yes, ma'am!"

The next morning, en-route for the meeting, Angelo awaited his train back to Oakland. He wished Phaedra had come with him, but she apparently thought it best Angelo go by himself. He and Alex were set to meet downtown at Frank Ogawa Plaza before heading to a bar serving as the setting for Alex's upcoming art show, an exhibit in which Angelo could possibly gain a feature spot, a first for him. So lost in anticipation, the train rumbled right past him, almost completely vanishing on the horizon before he could make a run for it. Now he would have to wait another twenty minutes for the next one. Fortunately, with the Bay's notorious transit woes Alex, as a fellow native, would most likely be understanding.

Alex started a new sketch, deciding to draw the scenery so that when the next train did arrive he wouldn't miss it. At some point an elderly black woman sat down on the bench next to him, and upon boarding the train she claimed the seat adjacent to his. He momentarily looked up from his sketch to offer a smile.

"That's a nice picture," the woman said.

Angelo lifted his head again, and let his eyes linger on the stranger this time. She might have been a little younger than Yiayia, though she seemed to carry herself with a similar regal grace. "Thank you, ma'am."

The woman smiled. "The art projects at the senior center were a highlight of my day. One time we had to bring in a family photo and make a sketch. I'll tell you, I stopped being able to recognize most people in my photo until I started drawing them. The memories came right back then."

"That's a nice story, ma'am. Would you like this picture?" Angelo asked, offering the sketch.

"That's so sweet of you. What a kind young man. I'm Betty, by the way."

"Good to meet you, Betty. I'm Angelo. In Greek, we have a word *philotimo*. Basically, it means generosity. Hospitality. I'm just passing it on." The woman's smile widened, her face brightening upon receiving the sketch. "Well, ma'am," Angelo continued, "this is 12th Street, my stop. Take care, and enjoy the art."

Via escalator, Angelo rose above ground amid Oakland's brick-and-pavement heart; Scrapers on four wheels cruising by those glass-and-steel skyscrapers lining the adjacent block. On the corner past De Lauer's Newsstand a lone man in a Warriors jersey, whom Angelo didn't recognize from yesterday's gentrification protest, leaned against a wall with the stem of his "WE GREW HERE, YOU FLEW HERE" sign jutting out from between his legs like a giant phallus. Initially, the man eyed Angelo as if to emphasize the sign's declaration. But then something in Angelo's posture caused a new brightness to flicker in the man's gaze. With a smile, he said, "Town Biz, what it is, youngster."

Angelo returned the grin. "Game recognize game in The Town."

Like a fallen acorn, beneath the city landmark that was the giant oak tree at Frank Ogawa plaza, Alex Kouros shifted among a small crowd, chatting and emphasizing his words with his hands. Upon closer glance, Angelo realized that he and Alex did resemble one another. They might have been mistaken for brothers, and boasting the same initials and the same penchant for the arts, it all seemed serendipitous.

After the crowd dispersed, Angelo strolled up with his hands in his pockets, a manila folder full of manuscript pages and random sketches tucked under an arm. Without gazing directly at Alex, whose eyes were trained on the phone in his lap, Angelo asked, despite already knowing the answer, "Are you Alex?"

Alex glanced up with a smile and pocketed his phone. Another one, initially unnoticed by Angelo, started ringing just as the one Alex had put away buzzed at his hip. "Sorry, brother. Non-stop grind, right? I'm Alex indeed. And you must be Angelo."

Angelo nodded and then found himself engulfed in a one-armed hug, barely having enough time to secure the folder against his chest as Alex pulled him close.

"Phaedra had some great things to say about you, brother. So, that's your girl, huh?" Angelo started to stammer a reply, but Alex cut in with, "She's a keeper, man, like a sister to me. Anyway, so tell me about this graphic novel. Shoot me your pitch."

Angelo launched into his concept with the velocity of a runway-rumbling jetliner. "So, my story's hero . . . The Greek . . . he's larger-than-life, real suave, a crime-fighting ladies' man with the power of the twelve Olympian gods at his disposal. He's fighting to preserve the heart of the city in a battle that seems unwinnable . . ."

Alex had a way about him, whether a certain stance or look in his eye, Angelo wasn't sure. However he did it, Alex made it seem as though he'd previously heard the story, already given it the green light, and was now simply basking in the joy of a repeat listen. By the time he finished talking, Angelo felt as though he had spoken his way into imminent good fortune.

"Now, that's *something*," Alex remarked with a glint in his eye, further fostering in Angelo a sense of optimism. "You've got a winner, for sure. So, I'm planning an art show. Musicians, painters, writers. Can I see your portfolio?"

Angelo handed over his folder, puffed his chest a little while watching Alex leaf through the drawings.

"Man, this is it. The *truth*, you know? The drawings have great energy, and sure, people have been incorporating Greek mythology into comics for a long time, but not like you. What do you say we make copies of some of these, blow them up about this big," Alex paused to spread his arms at a length approximately double the size of the current sketches, "and frame them on the wall of the bar? *Perfect*, I say. You never know *who* might come through, as many notable names as I'm inviting. Rickey Henderson, Mistah Fab, Michael Chabon. Might just find yourself with a publishing deal by night's end."

Angelo wanted to believe. And if he did, there wasn't much to lose. "That sounds perfect, man. Thanks for the opportunity!"

"No problem, brother. I'm shooting for the first Saturday of next month. That way we avoid getting swallowed among First *Friday* activities, but everyone will be immersed in the artistic vibe already. Let me show you."

They left Frank Ogawa Plaza, strolled up 14th Street and over to Jefferson, Alex discussing his role in the gentrification backlash, speaking about the impact of his TRUE TOWN tour and how he thought it more effective than the hyper-aggressive stance adopted by those choosing to go around with KILL A HIPSTER signs.

"Here we are," Alex said while indicating a business, TOWN TAVERN, that looked better suited as a bank than a bar with its tiled facade and columned doorway below what might have been apartments on the building's upper floors. The establishment was closed, evidently not an option for day drinkers, but Angelo moved to the window. A high archway above the bar counter even resembled a space suited for teller windows. "This is the spot," Alex continued. "I've been dreaming this up a good while, man. Most of my friends are artists, y'know? Ever heard that saying 'those who can't do, teach'? Well, in my case it's 'those who can't paint, promote.' In the arts community, I'm the negotiation man. Anyway, there's a stage near the back. People will read their poetry, short stories, sing and rap. Visual art—your art—will be framed up on the walls. A celebration of our city's creative visionaries. What's going to set it apart from other similar festivals, you ask? Well, the slogan's T.O.B. Talent Over Bullshit. The art scene is really clique-ish, you know? But this is anti-clique. It's about bringing everybody together. All these people coming from someplace else, out of state or wherever, they're just searching for home. Art is home, I say. So, it's official, right? I can put you on the list for sure?"

Angelo nodded. "Absolutely." This time, when that gleam came into Alex's eye, Angelo was ready for the one-armed embrace to follow.

Alex's phone rang. He checked the number, then regarded Angelo with an apologetic shrug. "I gotta take this. Hang on." Sure enough, his other phone buzzed soon after he took the call.

"So, why do you have two phones?" Angelo asked when Alex hung up.

Alex shrugged again. "Hustle double-time. Great meeting you, brother, but I've gotta run to the next thing."

"No problem."

Alone again, Angelo regretted not asking Alex what he thought about any potential confusion brought about by their names. In leafing through his drawing portfolio and coming across one of the early sketches from his graphic novel, he considered that he might just go by The Greek. Another piece caught his attention, this one a recent self-portrait. He studied it for a long time, and thought about the elderly woman, Betty, he had met that morning while waiting for his train. At last, he started toward home, striding in his eagerness to share news of the art show with his family. Throughout the BART ride and the walk up his block, he kept the portrait apart from the folder.

He entered the house. Yiayia sat propped at the dining room table, sipping one of her nutritional shakes and gazing absently into the foreground. For only an instant did Angelo worry about a repeat of last night's reaction. As he approached his grandmother, he initially saw her brow begin to furrow, eyes narrowing. Then he displayed his self-portrait drawing, holding it before his chest as though it was an image on his T-shirt. Yiayia's face brightened.

"Angelo," she said, "Where have you been all this time?"

Earth
tones

Dear Mr. Saropoulos,

While your talent is evident, and your artistic vision admirable, we at Clark & Lawrence Gallery of Oakland regret to inform you . . .

Pete didn't bother to stack the letter amongst the others overflowing his desk like a work-in-progress, the re-stuffed envelopes meticulously layered atop each other in a criss-cross sculpture; a towering tribute to his own failure. Beneath this dismal shrine, his actual project; a hybrid painting-collage of the famous Oakland cranes hoisting the Parthenon in Athens across a vast, blue acrylic ocean. He momentarily clutched his palette knife like a dagger above the canvas, and then dropped it.

In high school, Pete and his friend D'Andre Bryant called it "the vandal shuffle;" that longest of walks after leaving the car en-route to the bombing site with a backpack full of spray paint, the cans knocking against each other with the unmistakable clink of contraband. In those days, that sound sent Pete's heart soaring. Now the noise just made him feel old. Graffiti was a teenage pursuit. Only a select few taggers were able to, by their mid-twenties, ascend from side streets and rail yards to gallery walls.

But this evening Pete, brimming with frustration, regressed to spray-can expressions after a near decade hiatus.

He couldn't hit up the train yard. Its gravel, and weed-choked rails reminded him too much of D'Andre—rest in peace—so he instead chose an alley downtown. In the twilight, beneath the shadows cast by the towering Tribune building, Pete stood among those familiarly intoxicating aerosol fumes. Streaks of aqua-blue coated weathered brick, the spraycan a natural extension of his limb. "You, there! Stop!"

The voice sounded fairly young. Pete dropped the paint and froze, caught in a flashlight's scope. At his back, a chain-link fence with too much barbed wire to scale. He squinted into the glare. A rookie cop? But the beefy figure held no gun, and at his waist no bulge of a hip holster either. Pete slung the heavy backpack across his chest, and charged the light.

"I said, st—"

Pete heaved all his weight behind the backpack and bowled over the security guard. Like a downed trash can, the man hit the garbage-slick pavement, his flashlight clattering beyond arm's reach. Ready to bolt, Pete hesitated. In the searchlight's beam, the guard's face was a full moon glowing oddly familiar. Pete's breath burned in his throat as he dared a closer look. His eyes went round as the circles in the Krylon logo. "Todd-fucking-Mahoney? Ho, shit! Is that you?"

The guard lifted his mammoth head, and then wheezed to a sitting position before retrieving his lamp. "Who..."

"It's *me*. Pete. Pete the Greek. From high school, remember?"

"Well, got-damn," Todd panted. "Still the same no-account asshole who never grew up."

Pete knew he should just book it, but now things were personal. "What are you doing with your life that's so great, mister Rent-a-Justice?"

"What are you doing with *your* life?"

"What are you doing with—the hell with this!"

At last, Pete sprinted to the street. After triple checking that Todd Mahoney hadn't followed, he slowed to an inconspicuous stroll.

At a corner table in a Chinese restaurant, he contemplated a dish of shrimp fried rice while the blades of the overhead fan chased each other like cops after crooks. His tagging expedition didn't seem worth the risk now. In his demand to put work on display, to hell with a gallery, he'd only reminded himself that almost nobody cared about underground art—except to condemn it.

Closed to traffic, Telegraph on the following Friday evening, first of the month, literally swirled with color. Amid the various vendor booths lining the street, people took to the asphalt with multi-hued jumbo chalk. Further along, a quartet of elderly black men in matching pink vests-and-neckties crooned classic R&B tunes, the notes lilting above this carnival-of-sorts.

Cruising the cross street, a classic Oakland Scraper—1970's Chevy Nova—candy yellow and lifted on huge rims better suited for a covered wagon, rumbled along with a quaking bass-boom.

Pete stood on the sidewalk beside his buddy Alex Kouros, taking in the scene as they had many times. Tonight, however, Pete sensed a heaviness in his chest as though his heart descended along with the sun. The monthly Oakland Art Murmur felt more like a sigh.

"So, that's when I told the guy, 'What, do you want me to say it in Greek? Either get on board with the plan or don't.' Can't be much of an investor if you're afraid to take risks, right? . . . Right?"

Pete blinked. "Sorry, man. I kinda spaced there."

"What's with you tonight?"

Nearby, another cluster of people witnessed a seemingly impromptu breakdance battle. Pete fixated on one dancer poised single-footed on the back of a bus bench, arms outstretched as if for flight. "I'm wondering," Pete started again, "about the point of it all. If art doesn't make sense—if it doesn't make dollars—why so many new galleries downtown? Why are hipsters getting all the opportunities?"

Alex raised an eyebrow. "How do you mean?"

"I mean, this is great, but do the local artists really benefit? It seems like only out-of-towners are making money."

"To make money you have to really go out and push."

"Spare me the whole 'hustle' spiel tonight. I'm in my mid-twenties, and Jean-Michel Basquait was already an art powerhouse at twenty-one."

Alex spread his palms. "True, except didn't he die at twenty-seven?"

Pete didn't want to hear it. "Maybe the whole 'follow your dreams' thing tastes as much like bullshit as it sounds. Maybe art isn't my thing. Maybe I'm supposed to be doing something else, but it's too late."

Alex laughed. "But think about how many hipsters getting strangled by their own neckties want to be in *your* position, living their passion." Silent now, Alex stood with head high and dark eyes aglow. "Most people say, 'I'll be an artist after I retire,' but I say let your heart lead the way while you're young.' Now, you might think I'm full of shit, but can you argue with the wisdom of your dad?"

I can't be an art star, Pete thought, *and I can't be my dad, either.*

"Come on," said Alex, "let's grab some food."

Arranged in front of an apartment building, several canvases showcased pastel and acrylic portraits of working class characters—garbage men, grocers, school children, cops, mechanics: local color depicted in vibrant hues. Passerby—mustachioed hipsters; baseball cap-wearing hip-hoppers; middle-class couples in identical jogging attire—studied each piece, sharing smiles before maneuvering around Pete and Alex.

"I understand your point," Pete told Alex while waiting in line at a hotdog cart. "I don't think I want to do the art thing anymore."

"What you need is to get out of town. Escape the city and concrete and smog. When's the last time you went camping?"

Pete made a face. "Are you serious? Had to be in high school when we volunteered as counselors for church camp."

"That means we're due for a trip. What do you say next weekend we go to Point Reyes? Rough it like a couple Greek cowboys. If there is such a thing."

Pete shrugged. "If you really think us city folk can make it out there. I'm guessing you've still got some equipment?"

"Indeed."

The next Friday afternoon, Pete stood in Alex's driveway contemplating the open trunk of his car revealing a bundled tent, a pair of air mattresses, and a few grocery bags full of beer. Pete still couldn't imagine an air mattress competing with his own comforter. Before he could renege on the plan, however, Alex expounded on the merits of the trip, asking if Pete wanted to spend the weekend tinkering with his "fort of rejection slips." That was all it took for Pete to get in the passenger seat, and then they were out on the road with vintage Too $hort blasting on the stereo. It sounded clear to everyone in earshot that in leaving Oakland, the city would never leave them.

They cruised through Richmond, and across the San Rafael Bridge, then traveled 101 North for a few miles before taking a two-lane road west. Beyond his window the soothing palette of wildflowers, their golden petals vivid brushstrokes amid the green backdrop, almost made Pete forget why Alex had suggested they skip town.

If he was done with art, what *would* he do? As they passed a section of strawberry fields, Pete at least felt fortunate he wasn't among those stooped over in the sun plucking those little red hearts that bruised too easily.

They reached Point Reyes and parked at the campground, an expansive site amid lush pine trees reminiscent of Christmas, golden earth studded with foxtails, and a distant view of the beach accessible by one of the many rocky trails.

"Well, we made it," Alex said after he and Pete unloaded the gear. "Suppose we should celebrate with a couple beers?"

"Probably a good idea to set up the tent first," Pete suggested.

"If I can remember how."

"This trip was your idea!"

Alex spread his palms. "Doesn't mean I actually know what I'm doing." He jabbed a thumb at his chest, then added, "City boy, remember?"

With a sigh, Pete examined the components of the tent, and after a few false starts, had it built and ready.

"Just like putting a sculpture together, I bet," said Alex in observing the finished product.

Pete smiled.

"Now what?" Alex asked. "How about a round of cards?"

"Sure," said Pete.

By sundown, hunger set in. True, Alex packed more beer than food, though he hadn't skimped in regard to nourishment as they feasted on steaks and shrimp, steamed broccoli, and potatoes roasted on the little brick grill.

An hour or so after eating, they were lounging, with full bellies, on sleeping bags spread outside their tent while the fire burned at their feet. Pete cracked another beer to prolong his buzz, and Alex tuned his radio to a baseball game.

"Not so bad after all, right?" said Alex.

"Guess not," Pete replied.

Alex sipped a fresh beer of his own. "I'm thinking tomorrow morning we'll go for a hike, climb one of those hills and enjoy the view, then trek down to the water. Deal?"

"Sure," said Pete.

"You gotta admit this was a pretty solid idea. Don't try and tell me the fresh air hasn't already given you some inspiration."

Pete forced a smile. "Breathing better than ever."

"That's the spirit."

They finished their brews in silence, and Pete kept his gaze on the fire, mesmerized by its glow; the flicker of orange that lapped at the shadows like a thirsty tongue.

He dreamed of standing before a shut door, struggling with a massive key ring. One after the other he shoved the keys into the lock, fingertips rubbing raw against the serrated brass teeth, and each time he tried the knob it wouldn't budge. Then he peered over his shoulder where a fire raged at the bottom of the stairs. Its flames edged ever closer.

When he awoke to pale light filtering through the tent's fabric, he expected to find the campfire still smoldering, but a glimpse outside revealed only ashes. It couldn't have been much past dawn, the sky still retaining a purplish blush. He lay back down atop his air mattress. The one next to it was empty, no telling how long Alex had been up, though Pete couldn't see the point of rising so early if you didn't have to. At that moment it hardly seemed worth the effort to rise at all.

Despite what he had told his friend last night about feeling renewed via the rural breeze, a fitful sleep as a result of the strange, distant hoots and howls—in conjunction with his strange dream—left him sluggish. This day would mark the eighth in a row that he hadn't painted a fresh canvas, or tinkered with a work in progress. Now more than ever, amid the stillness of these unfamiliar surroundings, he felt that choice bearing down on him.

"Hey, you awake?" Alex asked, peeking into the tent.

Once outside, Pete received a mug of coffee strong enough to partially boost him free of his funk. Alex had prepared a feast of fried eggs and pancakes while their campfire was still burning.

"After we eat, we'll set off on that hike," Alex said, marching in place as pantomiming the advance of a true outdoorsman.

Pete sighed heavily. "I don't know, man . . ."

"C'mon, tackling nature is another kind of hustle, you just have to—"

"Alright, alright, jeez," Pete cut in, "I'll go."

Backpacks secured, water bottles in hand, they ascended a steep trail. Soil slid underfoot while they climbed, smoky dust clouds plumed in their wake as if they stomped out tiny fires with each step. Alex led the way, brushing back an occasional branch. Tangles of underbrush lined the path, deep green save for scattered bursts of orange and gold from tiny wildflowers. The air heavy with the scent of earth, dappled sunlight filtered down through the trees.

Pete's breath burned in his throat. He considered himself in fairly good shape, but a rural hike required a different stamina than a trek through the city. Still, he felt grateful for the excursion as it forced him out of his head. He kept his gaze on the backs of Alex's boots, the continual rise and fall motivating him to keep pushing despite the fatigue.

After rounding a bend, they marched in full sunlight again, emerging through the trees to scale a second hill. The trail gradually degraded into a finer silt rendering footing even more hazardous. They were flanked by tall, dry grass, but on the breeze Pete caught a hint of the ocean. At one point he nearly rammed into Alex, noticing almost too late that his friend had stopped and stood instead with his hand raised to signal silence. The trail was just wide enough for them to stand side-by-side, so Pete crept around to get a better view. Just up ahead, a pair of deer. The doe stood plucking at the weeds, her body a gentle slope amid the grass, auburn coat glowing in the tranquil light. Beside the doe, the fawn; a smaller version of her mother, with coat spotted white.

Pete kept still, holding his breath and counting the seconds while the animals remained unaware, or at least unbothered, by the presence of humans. Then the doe lowered her head, big black eyes meeting those of Pete, who found himself unable to look away. For a long moment the deer held his gaze, head tilted slightly, ears and tail twitching. Pete waited for her to move; either charge, or sprint in the opposite direction. But the animal kept stationary. The longer Pete stared into its eyes, the more he expected the encounter to be bestowed with meaning, as though the universe owed him a grand epiphany.

Then, another pair of fawns materialized amid the brush, pale spots barely visible atop their young coats. From the corner of his eye, Pete saw Alex standing as still as he, and equally uncertain. The doe stomped a forefoot, and in the next instant darted away through the foliage trailed by her offspring.

Pete and Alex climbed the path until they reached a cliff's edge and caught sight of the ocean, the white caps cresting and falling in a way that reminded Pete of seagulls diving for fish. Chest heaving, and legs burning, he stepped to the brink of the rocky precipice. He gazed at the shore some hundred feet below, the pristine sand a tawny band stretched toward the southern horizon. In the other direction, massive gray boulders tumbled amid the surf like the heads of giant harpies. Pete took another step, soil giving way underfoot to send pebbles plummeting beyond the margin. He had never been particularly fearful of heights, but in that moment his head swam with angst.

"Inspiring enough for you?"

At the sound of Alex's voice, Pete stepped back.

They descended the cliff via another slippery trail that sent dirt sliding to the point that they had to crouch in some places and scoot forward while grasping at the vegetation. They found a rocky cove sheltered from the gusts and caught their breath between gulps from their water bottles. From his pack Alex withdrew a container of trail mix and offered it to Pete.

"All bases covered, I see," Pete said after taking a palmful of the snack. "If I had just happened to meet you on one of these paths, marching along with your super-official gear, I'd find it hard to believe you were from mean, old Oakland."

Alex chuckled. "We know some parts are meaner than others. Besides, I don't have the damnedest clue about tying a square knot, or whatever."

The ocean tide's ebb and flow inspired a nostalgia in Pete, drawing him back to the past before pushing out to the present again. "Remember the night we met as kids, you and your folks came over to our place in San Ramon? Man, you were gawking around like that was the *country* or something."

Alex shrugged. "Suburbs, man. Almost the same thing to a city boy. Even a Greek one who'd already visited the *horyo* several times."

Pete's gaze remained distant. "I asked what you liked to do for fun, and you said 'draw.' Sure, I had scribbles up on my walls, but when we were kids I figured you would become the artist."

"Man, to have *your* gift for drawing, I'd trade all my talents away."

"Yeah, well," said Pete, "all it's gotten me is a few pats on the back and fairly empty pockets."

"Still on a downer, huh? Even out here, far from the city, far from the "art scene" that seems to be depressing you, for whatever reason?"

Pete lowered his gaze. His chest felt tight. Worse was the sinking sensation of self-pity, but he didn't know how to rise above it.

"Man, you know well as I that a ton of people admire your stuff," Alex said. "Those who don't? Fuck 'em. Nothing's for everybody. But if you're *that* down-and-out, it might not really be what you want after all. Don't quit and then sit back with regrets, though."

Pete looked once more at the horizon where a sailboat tacked against the sky as if bound for the heavens. He shaded his eyes against the sun as the vessel disappeared beyond the massive rocks.

A gaze back toward the sandy outcropping from which they had descended revealed a hawk circling the clouds; a fanned smudge of black against the pantone background. Then Pete noticed something else. Another silhouette, this one human and standing at the edge. The figure took an unsteady step forward, as Pete himself had done earlier atop the crag. However, this stranger went so far as to dangle one foot off the edge, Pete's breath catching in his throat as the silhouette wobbled on one leg for an instant before readjusting its stance.

"What's he doing?"

Alex shrugged. "Looks a little suspicious, whatever it . . ." He let his voice trail off as the distant figure leaned over raised on tip-toes, catching himself just before he toppled.

Pete exchanged a glance with his friend before they wordlessly dashed for the cliff. Flushed and panting, he and Alex soon reached the top. The stranger stood with his back to them, clad in a faded hoodie and tattered jeans, arms spread wide as though to worship the sun. His hair, the color of spare change, danced in the wind like frayed thread and added to the overall impression—at least in Pete's mind—that he, just like his outfit, was slowly coming apart.

Perhaps it was best they keep quiet and retreat down the path. But then the man took several steps backward before moving toward the cliff's edge again, his determined stride suggesting that he might launch himself this time.

Alex charged, crashing atop the stranger who writhed in his grasp, kicking and hollering. They rolled around in the dirt just a yard or so from the edge, until Pete yanked them apart. The man looked less disheveled from the front: his face clean-shaven and younger than expected—Pete estimating him early forties—with clear blue eyes and a forehead free of lines.

"There we go, nice and easy," Alex said, clutching the stranger's arm. "Maybe this is all for show, but you sure seemed serious about that jump. I'm Alex, and this is my buddy, Pete. Now you know our names, so you can think of us as friends. What's your name, friend?"

The man didn't answer, his eyes flicking with a hawkish intensity from Alex to Pete, limbs twitching as if in anticipation of flight, despite Alex's grip.

In the following quiet, Pete heard only the steady huff of his own breath. Then the stranger spoke.

"My name is Douglas."

"Okay, Douglas," Alex said, slowly, after exchanging another glance with Pete. "What were you planning to do?"

Douglas contemplated the precipice and simply said, "Jump." The man's face was childlike in its lack of calculation. "I don't want to be here anymore."

"You don't mean that—"

Douglas cut in before Alex finished. "You don't know shit about me. You're not my friends, I don't have any friends."

Alex spread his palms. "I'm sorry. It's true, we don't know anything about you, but we'd like to. You were alone just a while ago, but now you've met two people who don't want to see anybody get hurt. Let's forget about what you were planning to do, okay? We'll start simple. So, we're from Oakland. Where are you from?"

Douglas gazed at the sky. "I'm from Shasta."

Alex raised his eyebrows. "The far north, huh? Beautiful country up there. Believe it or not, I have a real good friend whose grandma was born on a train in Redding. Small world, huh?"

"Guess so."

"And what brought you down this way?"

"I needed an escape."

"Like a vacation?" Alex asked.

"No. Like a getaway."

Alex frowned. "Is someone after you?"

A shadow passed over Douglas's face. "Three weeks ago . . . I killed my brother! I was drunk and driving the goddamn car."

Through clenched teeth, Pete took a deep breath. He checked his phone in case he needed to call for help. The battery was charged, but no signal.

"I'm really sorry to hear that," said Alex.

Douglas nodded. "We were only a year apart, raised in foster care together. He was all I had, and now he's gone."

Things went quiet for a time, and then Alex said, "I won't bullshit you and play like I understand what you're going through, Douglas, because

I don't. But know there are people here to listen."

"My brother was *everything* to me," Douglas said, his voice breaking.

"My life doesn't seem to be working out either, and a year ago I lost my brother, too." Pete spoke for the first time, and both Alex and Douglas regarded him with surprise. He noticed Alex shoot him a puzzled glance, but ignored it and cycled through his phone photos, holding up for Douglas an image featuring a graffiti mural-portrait of D'Andre Bryant, Pete's cherished high school friend and fellow artist. "He was my friend, my teacher . . . the risk taker I always wanted to be."

D'Andre's face was rendered in rich browns, dark oranges, subtle yellows and greens, grayish-blue near the crown of his head as if to suggest a somber sky. Deep earth tones chosen to commemorate the autumn season when D'Andre had, apparently, taken his own life.

"Who painted that?" asked Douglas.

"I did," Pete replied. "He's gone, never forgotten."

"He looks . . . black," said Douglas. "I mean, he's lots of colors in this painting, except . . . well, you know what I mean."

"So, he wasn't my biological brother," Pete clarified, "but I had love for him just the same."

Douglas gestured for the phone. Pete handed it over and watched as Douglas studied the screen.

"I wish I'd had the talent to honor my brother like that. But I can't do anything right. I lost my job . . . I lost it all."

Pete said, "Tell you what, Douglas. I'll promise to help pay artistic tribute to your brother. How's that sound?" A long shot, but it appeared the only one he would have. Pete held his breath, listened to the distant waves.

Douglas was silent a moment, then nodded. "I hope you follow through on that promise."

"Absolutely."

"Why don't you come to our campsite for some lunch," said Alex. "Speaking of food, we own a food truck back in Oakland. We could use extra help. Can you cook?"

"Not really. But I know engines."

"Well, the truck could use a tune up, and I've got a friend who has his own shop. He's looking to hire."

Douglas smiled. "What's for lunch?"

That evening back in Oakland, after dropping Douglas off at the auto shop, Alex and Pete rolled toward home.

"I'm feeling optimistic about Douglas," Alex said.

"Me, too," replied Pete. "I'll check up on him in a few days."

"So, you feeling better?"

Pete looked thoughtful. "You know, in that mural of D'Andre, the earth tones are so on point." "

"So, what's next?"

"Not totally sure. Tomorrow I think I'll buy new paint."

Sacrificial Lamb

At three-thirty on Easter morning, as he halted at a stoplight, Alex Kouros caught the attention of a cop in the adjacent lane, the patrolman furrowing his brow at the ruddy phosphorescence emanating from Alex's lap. Alex lifted his candle with its red plastic wax receptacle. The cop's face melted into a scowl, as though Alex's flame was misdemeanor-worthy. But when the light changed, the cruiser rolled on. Afterward, Alex considered that the candle glow, if not unlawful, may have been taken as a personal affront.

A week earlier, eighteen-year-old Victor Jamison had been shot dead over an iphone mistaken for a gun by the Oakland Police Department. In the wake of his murder, people marched the streets in BLACK LIVES MATTER T-shirts, their fists cradling candles as they shouted, "You can take my life, but you won't diminish my light!" Oakland—like New York, Baltimore, Chicago, and other cities—had been cast in the media's glare as a "sudden hotbed of tension between residents and law enforcement" as though hostility toward police simply ignited one day like dry earth after a single spark. Following Victor's death, cops weren't huge fans of candles.

Alex regarded his candle again, recalling how during the midnight service the lights were deadened. In shadow, the priest descended his altar to offer the initial flame. One by one, parishioners ignited each other's wicks until the entire church glowed with new life. A single spark had conquered the darkness. Now, Alex pulled into his driveway and adjusted his candle's crown, determined to enter the house without diminishing the tiny blaze. Fresh from *Anastasee* services, belly full of the *magiritsa* soup eaten in the wee hours following liturgy to break the forty-day Lenten fast, he felt sluggish in the driver's seat. He raised the volume to catch a snippet of yet another radio interview with the main fighter for justice in Victor Jamison's death, Ms. Regina Parker.

"*. . . What we have is yet another case of a young, black teenager brutally murdered at the hands of forces supposedly sworn to serve and protect.*"

"*But Missus Parker, what is your response to people pointing out that Victor Jamison, though merely eighteen-years-old, possessed a rap sheet that ran back to pre-adolescence? He has arrests from the age of twelve for petty crimes, plus more serious charges over subsequent—*"

Alex cut the radio off. In the new silence, he could picture Ms. Parker; long-time local combatant of police brutality whose helmet-like natural updo in combination with her customary urban camouflage gave her an inner-city soldier persona.

The world may have been falling apart, but with the rising sun, on the Holy Pascha, Alex felt that things would be okay again. Exiting the car, Alex ascended his front steps, mindful of the candle flame, and noticed a glow in a window next door. The neighbors, a youngish couple named the Richardsons, had migrated a few weeks prior from Wisconsin—or was it Minnesota? They seemed pleasant enough until Alex said too much on that Sunday afternoon a week earlier. Alex, in his sleek Chevy, and Cal Richardson, in his boxy Chrysler, pulled into their respective driveways at the same moment. Like an insistent lullaby, the snoozy jazz from Cal's car droned louder as if to pacify Alex's KPFA listenings.

"In the days prior to Victor's murder, the police had been called, by a family not from Oakland, mind you. They said there were suspicious of—"

Alex had lowered the volume upon expecting the usual neighborly greeting. Still, he could hear the radio debate in his head.

"How goes it, friend?" Cal Richardson asked. "Any Easter plans for next weekend?"

"Well, I'm Greek Orthodox, so it's a big holiday for us..."

"Really?" Cal asked, tugging on the strings of his windbreaker as if in his relocation he had brought along the gusts of a Midwestern spring. "A big holiday, you say? How's that?"

Cal's blue eyes had reminded Alex of spring pastels, and the traditions that accompanied those gentle tones: chocolate bunnies and egg hunts. Feeling like the rain on Cal's picnic, Alex stormed in with: "This will be my first year hosting the party. I'm going to roast a lamb in the backyard."

"Is that so?" Cal Richardson had asked, mouth contorted in a queasy grimace as if Alex had just confessed a propensity toward human sacrifice. To Alex, standing on the sidewalk between his house and the Richardsons', the pavement suddenly seemed twice as wide.

"Yes," Alex said. "It's Easter tradition in our culture."

"You're going to cook an *entire* lamb right out there on the grass?" Cal asked while long shadows slanted across his doughy face to mask the full extent of his apparent displeasure.

Alex nodded. "A friend of mine, also Greek, has a plot of sheep down in Modesto. Have you never tried lamb?"

Cal cleared his throat. "June and I are pescatarian. We just love that fish market down the block."

"Oh, the new place. Used to be a family-owned bakery in that spot, but they got priced out. Anyhow, if you decide to come over we'll have plenty of meatless side dishes but no seafood, unfortunately."

Cal managed a stiff smile. "Good to know."

On the Richardsons' front porch, Cal's wife, blonde and bright-eyed, materialized like a divine intervention.

"Alex, you remember my better half, June."

"Hello, Ms. Richardson."

"Please," said Cal's wife, "call me June. Where we come from everyone is considered a neighbor, whether you live next door, down the block, or all the way across town." June descended the steps to join Alex and Cal on the sidewalk. "We're people people," she continued, "and, truthfully, I'm a little worried about my lovey Cal here."

"*June . . .*" Cal grumbled.

Alex had suppressed a chuckle.

"See, we're good folk," June went on, "and good folk attract the like, but Cal's been having trouble making friends since we moved here on account of the new job."

"Dairy industry not what it used to be?" Alex asked.

"Cal's father worked with cheese, but Lovey's always been into computers. Anyhow, I just pray he'll connect with someone and enjoy a little guy-time apart from his IT duties. Why don't you join us for dinner tonight?"

"Oh, thank you, but—"

June's face resembled that of an unpopular child anticipating the rejection of her sleepover invite. Alex forced a smile. "Sure, why not?"

"Great!"

When Alex arrived for dinner later that evening, it seemed to take double the normal time to reach the Richardsons' front steps. If only Alex had left it at "having a barbecue" rather than revealing the guest of honor; a marinated lamb carcass that would, when bound to the spit, somewhat resemble a crucifixion.

The homey scent of fresh-baked bread lured Alex past the entryway. Adorning the white walls, framed photos of the Richardsons. Some might have said they looked like siblings, though there was no true resemblance apart from the blue eyes and the platinum-blonde hair. Whether positioned in front of a Christmas tree, the old Metrodome, or the entrance to Jack London Square in matching I HEART OAKLAND shirts, Cal and June retained an identical pose.

"Please, Alex, have a seat." June came in from the kitchen with a pitcher of lemonade.

"Would you also like some wine, Alex?" asked Cal. "We do have a bottle currently aerating on the counter."

"Not quite yet, thanks."

"Sorry we don't have any meat for you," Cal remarked upon taking his seat.

"No need to apologize. I go meatless plenty nights. I'm just grateful to have been invited over."

"Thank you, Alex, we're happy to have you," said June. "Lovey, you must have noticed Alex drives a Chevy, too. Weren't you looking for parts? Maybe he knows a good shop around town."

Cal gulped lemonade. "Honey, I drive a Chrysler. And I found a place down on Broadway."

"Maybe you guys can still talk cars, y'know, like you used to do with the boys back home . . ."

The muscles in Cal's jaw bulged, and he chewed his salad as though it were something far more toothsome. "The tomatoes are from our little garden. I don't think we have as much yard space as you, surely not large enough to roast an animal . . . if we were into that sort of thing. But we make do. Next course, in the slow cooker, is a vegetable stew, and we'll finish off with broiled salmon. Hope you're hungry."

"You bet. How long have you been veg—er—pescatarian? I hear overfishing is a real environmental problem."

"We've been proud pescatarians for the last twelve years. June and I were both raised on your typical meat-and-potatoes Midwestern diet, but then I caught testicular cancer. No real evidence that the two were related, but I still decided to adopt a new way of eating."

"Cal got really sick," June added, "but the doctors found it early and he's been cancer free for over a decade."

"Congrats."

"Thanks," said Cal. "As June mentioned earlier, I grew up on a dairy farm, and only after illness did I realize the negative ramifications of that industry on animals and the earth in general."

"Cancer really changed Cal's outlook," said June, "we value all life, but those of animals especially now."

Cal gnawed at another forkful of salad. "Forgive me for saying this, but that's partly the reason we view your Easter plans as quite barbaric."

Alex sipped lemonade and wished he'd taken Cal up on the wine offer. "That's quite a strong word. Fish feel pain too, you know?"

"Now, I don't want to stomp on your traditions," Cal plowed on, "and I'll admit my ignorance of Greek culture despite the large population in the Midwest, but we're straight shooters."

"I respect that," Alex said, feeling more defensive than honored at the moment. "I guess we'll agree to disagree. For the record, I value animal lives a great deal, too. I've never supported hunting for sport, and Greek culture, being one of shepherds, has historically had a deeper bond with livestock than most Americans can understand."

"Why don't we talk about something else?" June asked.

Alex took a bite of salad. Then he remarked, "A real shame what happened to that kid."

Cal raised an eyebrow. "Which one is that, now?"

"Victor Jamison, the eighteen-year-old who was killed by the cop last night? Talk about a barbaric act."

Cal seemed to consider, then said, "Hot topics always make the breakroom rounds. Funny no one mentioned it. Anyhow, we can't rush to judge. Police are under enormous stress and risk their lives for us everyday. An eighteen-year-old is hardly a kid, you realize? I suspect we don't know the full story."

Excuse me, but I don't see the point in once again running through this young man's list of mistakes. I'm never one to perpetuate the idea that society is to blame for all problems. No, Victor Jamison made poor choices in the past, and faced the resulting consequences . . .

Alex took a deep breath, then simply asked Jane to pass the stew.

Four-thirty am.

Above the kitchen sink, after Father Stavropoulou's service, Alex fitted the lambatha into a spiral-shaped holder gifted to him by his father one Christmas. The *Pascha* candle stood proud before the window now, light oozing through the cone to christen the glass with a bloody hue. Every year, a fresh beginning; each Easter a new candle in honor of the rebirth.

Through his kitchen window, Alex glimpsed into the Richardsons' dining room. From their Jack London Square portraits, the couple stared back at him, their twin grins almost sinister in the shadows. Then Cal appeared next to the pictures, gazing in Alex's direction so that for one long, surreal moment Alex was confronted by his neighbor both in photograph and in real-time. Cal turned away before switching off the light.

Alex did the same, standing alone for an instant amid the candle's glow.

The Richardsons were still bothered, beyond reason it seemed, by Alex's plans to roast an Easter lamb. Maybe he would have heeded their concern were there not an adequate fence separating the properties; was the couple forcibly exposed to the sight of meat cooking over a spit. But the entire ritual would take place, effectively, behind closed doors.

Along the garage lay a yellow-and-black cooler the size of an industrial fridge, like a giant tool box, or, as the Richardsons would probably describe it upon viewing the contents, a coffin. Alex lifted the cooler lid. Atop the ice, rested the twenty-seven pound lamb; a perfect specimen of flesh and fat marbled pink-and-white beneath the overhead lamps. Alex hefted it onto a plastic-covered table, then returned to the kitchen for the basting mixture. Lights again shone in the Richardsons' window, but no sign of the couple. Back in the garage, while readying his marinade, Alex clicked on the stereo. Through the speakers, another snippet of Ms. Parker making the KPFA rounds:

"... While we are so ready to highlight Victor's faults, I wonder why we aren't as quick to mention his accolades, reminding everyone that in the last three to four years he made big strides in turning his life around. At the time of his murder Victor was working at a grocery store, attending community college classes..."

Alex checked the clock. Quarter to five. No sleep tonight since he hoped to get the lamb over the coals by seven, and ready to serve around noon. Still, he didn't feel as tired as expected. Too great was the anticipation of the Easter feast, and the resonating power of Father Stavropoulou's closing sermon.

Last night, Father had mentioned Victor Jamison, and requested prayers for his family and all others across the city whose lives had been cut short. The priest didn't discuss details of the incident—no mention of the police—but in acknowledging the death, Father Stavropoulou had given it a certain significance not lost on Alex.

"...*Lest we forget, Mister Taylor,*" Ms. Parker's voice punched onward through the radio speaker like a closed fist, "*Victor Jamison was unarmed at the time of the shooting. He wasn't committing a crime, and, furthermore, his moral character really has nothing to do with the facts of his unjust murder. Victor was simply a young man walking down a street near his home when officers began harassing him. Police claim they thought he had a weapon, but witnesses say Victor held only a cell phone. Even if he had been holding a pistol, why no call to drop it? Why just open fire on a teenager weighing a mere one-hundred-sixty-five pounds?*"

"*Point made, Missus Parker. We're running short on time. You're holding another rally later this morning, despite it being Easter Sunday, correct?*"

"*Yes. Eleven o'clock sharp, this morning, Easter Sunday and all. We'll be marching from 35th and International, the spot of Victor's death, to City Hall. Victor Jamison will not be another sacrificial lamb in this—*"

Alex switched his boombox to CD mode and loaded a *Bouzoukia* disc in hopes of again finding the holiday spirit as he adorned the meat with marinade, careful to get in all the corners and crevices until the flesh glistened, and the entire garage resonated a tangy, spice-rich aroma.

When the rising sun blushed through the windows, Dino arrived to help Alex secure the lamb on the spit. He insisted on tackling the contraption himself, making a show of tying the lamb to the rod with thick wires so that during roasting the legs wouldn't fall loose. Next they tended to their pit, stacking bricks—the edges biting into the tender flesh behind

Alex's knuckles—until they had an enclosure, about five feet wide and one foot high, with wood and charcoal in the center. Alex lit the fire, and they watched it grow as if through sheer observation they could coax it to full strength.

"Jimmy says the lambs follow him around the farm down there," Alex said, "almost like dogs."

"*Megalo einai toh arni, eh? Theenatoh,*" Dino remarked.

"Those babies get babied up until it's their time. He loves them. Must be hard to get down to business."

"Jimmy understands their sacrifice," Dino explained in Greek. "His family comes from a shepherd stock. Yes, he loves them, but it is a love most outsiders will never comprehend. Their innocent death is an intimate one; the result of a knife, not a gun. The lamb's blood nourishes the earth as its flesh nourishes the body. Its offering is not in vain."

As the flames rose within the red brick enclosure, Alex imagined one giant Easter candle ablaze. For an instant he thought he heard cries of protest on the breeze, but it was nothing more than hollow wind.

By ten-thirty, guests began to gather in the yard; a half-dozen friends nursing morning beers and orbiting ever closer to the heat of the roasting pit. No Greeks among the current crowd, but that didn't surprise Alex given his people's propensity to show up late, especially on Easter Sunday. Unlike the *Amerikani*, they knew to conserve their energy for the celebration to come. This was no baked-ham-and-egg-hunt afternoon, but rather a raucous affair of *tsipouro* shots, and *Kalamatiano* circle dances, and joyfully thunderous declarations of *Christos Anesti!* Heaven help the neighbors, along the entire block, should they choose not to join the festivities. Alex hadn't seen any trace of the Richardsons.

"*Piah einai aftee ee yehnaika pou menee deepla sou?*" Niko asked as Alex strolled up to check on the meat. "*Filandeza prepi na einai. Omorfee.*"

In pondering the question posed by Uncle Niko, ever the aging lothario, Alex tried to guess which woman Uncle was referring to. But when Niko added, "She must be Finnish. Beautiful," Alex figured June was the female in question given her blonde hair and Nordic features. Niko had apparently glimpsed her in the window.

Alex chuckled at the knowledge that uncle Niko, a true *kamaki* despite his advancing age, no doubt plotted to land a prized beauty of Northern European descent like so many Mediterranean players before him.

"She's married," Alex replied, "and even if she was single, I'm not sure you'd want to go down that road. She's pescatarian."

Niko made a face. "What I care if she work with sick dogs?"

"No, *pes*—never mind."

Niko just shrugged his broad shoulders and went back to turning the rod. Alex glanced toward the Richardson house, but still spotted no movement within.

Amid its steady churn on the spit, the lamb darkened over the flame, slowly adopting a rich, mahogany hue while his father, manning the end of the rod opposite uncle Niko, periodically basted it with the leftover marinade. Alex watched the revolution, round and round atop the open flame, until his eyes went out of focus. Only a vague brown shape remained; a body sacrificed in the name of *Thayo*.

As the sun reached its apex amid the clouds, the Greek contingent arrived, laughing and playfully chiding one another in the mother tongue. The lamb shone a fuller brown now with the promise of a tasty crust, and carving would soon commence. In the distance Alex heard someone from Ms. Parker's march bellow into a megaphone, "You won't diminish our light!"

"*Christos Anesti!*"

When his ten-year-old cousin Manoli came charging up wielding a hard-boiled egg dyed brilliant red, Alex readied one of his own. "Alithos Anesti!" he proclaimed in return.

Game on.

Manoli knocked his egg against Alex's. Only Manoli's specimen remained undamaged. "*Bravo sou, re*," Alex said. "You win. Now go try it with *Thea* Maria." He watched the boy run off across the grass, then pondered the egg between his fingers; the crimson shell splintered with tiny white cracks.

In online photos—pictures the public wasn't meant to see—the dead teen was a vague heap crumpled atop the asphalt like a pile of clothing, discarded. In the close-ups, however, the detail turned Alex's stomach. Those spaces along Victor's torso where bullets entered had reminded Alex of Greek Easter eggs; perfect red ovals torn in the brown flesh. Alex quickly peeled his egg now, eager to rid his mind of the association and reach the soft goodness beneath.

Dino made a show of twirling his knife prior to carving the lamb atop a picnic table near the pit, the tender meat sending spirals of steam skyward as thirty or so guests lined up with paper plates in hand. After Alex loaded his own platter with *arni* and the plentiful accompaniments, he joined his uncles at the table where they had gathered to eat and sip homemade *raki* poured from recycled water bottles.

In the heat of the afternoon, their unbuttoned shirts revealed golden crucifixes among their chest hair like charms atop puffs of cotton. Alex chose to sit with them knowing that they wouldn't speak of current events, at least not those related to local news. Instead their talk consisted of old country politics, their banter in the mother tongue transporting Alex to a place far away, reviving in his mind pleasant memories of sea waves crashing shoreline.

By sundown, the party's energy somewhat dwindled as guests sat digesting in the contemplative shadows of dusk, waiting out the twilight lull until ready to eat and dance anew. As Alex sat with eyes on the horizon, nursing a cozy buzz brought on by the plentiful food and drink, he initially assumed the knocking sound was only in his head; the echo of booze sloshing in his belly, if not simply the thud of a background instrument from the *laiko* flowing through the boombox speakers.

"You won't diminish our light!" Again, the voice, closer now, through the megaphone.

But it was the persistent knocking, not the shouted mantra, that sent him toward the fence. Upon opening the gate he frowned at the sheer predictability of their arrival. They stood, initially as shadowed silhouettes. Then, stepping into the light of the flood lamp, their dual tow-headedness shone bright as twin moons.

"You won't..."

"Oh, hey," Alex said, "you decided to join the festivities after all? Hope we aren't being too loud." Alex followed their gazes to where the lamb still rested on the spit, merely a picked carcass now. If they were bothered, their faces didn't show it.

"...diminish our light!"

"It's not the volume as much as the smell," snapped Cal. "Anyhow, we're just coming by to give you something to think about."

"We hope you'll take a look at this," June added, holding out a home-made pamphlet with colorful fruits and vegetables pictured amid a lush garden eden scene with Cal and June's photos arranged like portraits of Adam and Eve.

"You won't diminish our light!"

As the literature rustled in June's offered hand, Alex gazed into the night. In hopes of avoiding further disruption to his party, he ushered the Richardsons toward the sidewalk. The couple turned their heads toward the street, too. Through the darkness, like a battalion on the march, emerged a crowd with raised fists, candles flickering in their grip bright as fallen stars. The Richardsons side-stepped helplessly, unable to avoid nearly getting swallowed by the wave of protesters. The black man in lead, decked out in the same golden yellow color as the T-shirt worn by Victor on that tragic evening, held to his chest a photograph of the fallen teen like a superhero's emblem.

Alex pushed past Cal and June to edge closer to the brigade before it passed. Beside him, little Manoli appeared holding his *Pascha* candle, alight in the darkness. He offered it to Alex. Alex raised the candle high above his head. In the instant it took the protest leader to return the gesture, a helicopter roared overhead, blades slicing the wind as it circled wide. Before Alex could secure it, the pamphlet slid from June's grasp and twirled amid the wind like scrap, spinning so high it seemed unlikely to ever come down.

Bounce house

In silence, through the back gate, Angelo and Phaedra arrived at the festivities. With hands across brows they shielded their eyes from the slanting sun, and then, as if partially blind among the lengthening shadows, wandered separately through the crowd. Angelo didn't recognize anyone at first, but eventually found his friends. They stood faced away from him on the lawn, beer bottles in hand, twilight reflecting off the amber glass in tiny yellow asterisks while smoke from the barbecue grill billowed lazy punctuations overhead. Four buddies enjoying a Saturday out in the yard. Near the fence stood a bounce house, the giant inflated castle complete with a plastic drawbridge, bucking to-and-fro with the momentum of bodies vaulting within.

"Koutouvalis! *Ela tho!*"

Angelo turned at the sound of his hollered surname. Mike Lagounis strode across the grass with baby in arms, the boy sporting a pale blue T-shirt declaring "Now I'm 1!" and a lop-sided, chocolate-frosted grin. Angelo offered a wrapped box in exchange for a bottled beer, clinking it against the one Mike held.

"Glad you could make it out," Mike said. "After Alex's party, last week—or was that two weeks ago?—and the bar-hopping on Thursday night, I figured you'd need a break."

Angelo extended his index finger, and the baby's tiny hand closed around it. "You know I couldn't miss Yianni's big day." Then, indicating the baby's face, he added, "but did I miss the blowing out of the candles?"

Mike chuckled, wiping at his son's mouth with a damp napkin. "Nah, he grabbed a chunk of cake just now as we were walking across the kitchen. So, where's your girl?"

"Good question. She's been in a mood all day, that's why we're late. Let me go find her."

Phaedra stood near the yard entrance, the ivy hanging in rapids above her like a green avalanche. Sunlight cast through her dark hair, illuminating the finest strands with an otherworldly glow. Angelo waited for her to meet his gaze, but her attention was swayed by a tow-headed toddler. The child ambled up offering a clump of grass. Phaedra hugged her elbows defensively and stepped back. Finally, she patted the little girl's head.

When they at last met up by the cooler, Angelo, rummaging through the ice for a second beer, side-eyed Phaedra. She stood with arms crossed over chest. Was she playing aloof, or protecting herself? Was it something he said, or didn't say? "Hey, everything all right?"

Phaedra brushed a lock of hair behind her ear, the corners of her mouth jutting upward as though momentarily tugged by strings. "Sure. You get a chance to catch up with all the guys yet?"

The edges of Angelo's bottle cap bit into his palm before he realized it required an opener. "I've only seen Mike so far."

"Well, we just got here. Go ahead and mingle."

Angelo opened his mouth to test the potential reasons behind Phaedra's mood. But instead he simply muttered, "Will do."

"Well, brother," said Alex, tilting his Mythos bottle in Mike's direction, "you didn't have any material in the Town Biz Art Fest, but now it's showtime for you!"

Mike waved a playful hand. "I didn't want to steal the shine, that's all."

Everyone laughed.

As though unable to resist an inherent tribal urge, the Greeks all gathered at one of the plastic tables arranged off to the side with a full view of the lawn, and the bounce castle, and the general festivities where clustered guests chatted and drank. Angelo sat tugging at the label of his Pacifico—Alex Kouros and Pete Saropoulos flanking him, Johnny Eliopoulos and Mike Lagounis seated across the way.

"Bravo, Mikey L," Alex said, raising his bottle again. "You did it, big guy. Father to a beautiful boy."

Mike raised his drink. "Aw, shucks!"

Conducting their own cheers apart from the larger group, everyone at the table clinked bottles and drank deep. Angelo kept his gaze on the bounce castle jaunting with increased vigor while dizzy children stumbled in and out like drunken royalty. "A whole year gone already, huh? Hard to believe."

"Harder to believe you and Phaedra have already been together that long," Mike said. "Thanks to her, we were all introduced around the time little Yianni was born."

"Angelo, before you know it," said Alex, taking another hit of his beer, "we'll be celebrating your baby's birthday."

Angelo's cheeks went hot. He tried to focus on the bounce house, but the booze had already fuzzied his vision. "I don't know about that..."

"Gotta give 'em time to marry first," said Pete. "Phaedra's not the kids-out-of-wedlock type."

"Yeah," added Johnny, "and I'll be your wedding singer at a discount, bro."

While everyone else laughed, Angelo drained his beer and thought about escaping in pursuit of another.

From out of his pocket, Mike snagged a set of keys with a tiny charm shaped like a baby bottle, the name YIANNI engraved in blue letters. Disconnecting the charm from the ring, he steadied it between two fingers in the center of the table. "Okay, guys, little variation on spin the bottle. Whoever's targeted after the spinning stops is due to become a father next year."

Pete Saropoulos made a face. "Says who?"

"Courtney played a variation of this at her shower."

"Shouldn't it stay a game between women then?"

Without another word, Mike gave the keychain a whirl. At last, the charm stopped spinning and triggered a collective crash of chairs as everyone, save for Mike and Angelo, simultaneously sprang up from the table in an attempt to dodge assumed fate. Angelo wasn't all that surprised to find the bottle's tiny nipple jutting toward his chest.

"Congrats, friend," said Alex. "We owe you cigars."

"Maybe we'll even pitch in with a few diapers," Pete remarked.

"C'mon, guys," Angelo said, "mothers do all the work, right?" Then, with a laugh, he added, "fatherhood can't be that complicated."

"Yeah, since Mike finally took a shot at it, right?" said Johnny.

Mike laughed. "Johnny Eliopoulos, the R-and-B singing sensation! You're one to talk, bro. Your folks have been on you for years about settling down. First, the issue was hopping between too many beds, and then beds being off-limits with that 'Date-a-Dandy' escort gig. Ha!"

Johnny shrugged. "Happens all the time: a musician finally settles down, and the music goes to shit. He's got less struggle to inspire his songs. That won't be my story anytime soon. No woman's gonna gentrify me, believe it."

Pete looked thoughtful. "Johnny's got a point. I'd like to have kids. Someday. But it comes down to choosing a grind. Artist or father? Right now I can't imagine anything competing for my art time."

When the other guys went off to refresh their beverages or simply make the rounds, Angelo remained at the table. He contemplated the bounce castle again, envisioning an actual house thrusting about with the same force, propelled by adults scrambling off the walls in an attempt to get a grip on their newly domesticated lives.

The yard grew dark, guests milled about in scattered pairs; couples stealing tipsy kisses amid the shadows. Angelo felt the warmth of fingers along the back of his neck, and detected lavender perfume behind him. Phaedra came up out of nowhere, her hands massaging his shoulders now. "Hey, stranger," Angelo said. "Have a seat."

"Hey," Phaedra replied, not moving. "You boys looked busy with your beers and your toy. I didn't want to butt in."

"Toy? Oh, the bottle charm." Angelo reached to take Phaedra's arm, gently pulling her in front of him. "We were playing a game. Guess I'll be a daddy next year." Phaedra's jaw may have tightened for an instant, but Angelo wasn't sure.

"Congrats," she said, "who's the baby momma?"

Angelo knew it was probably best to play along, but he felt a nagging sensation in his throat, a certain tickle in need of clearing. "Since you introduced me to the guys, I feel . . . it's like they've got their stuff together, families and all, and it seems great. Grown up, you know?"

"So, you want what they have."

Angelo sighed as a vague frustration rose in his chest. "I get that it's only been a year, but we've talked about the future . . ."

"Sure," said Phaedra. "It's fun to dream."

"Okay, so why do you get so weird whenever I mention kids?"

Phaedra sat straighter in her chair. "Because we've already discussed children, and my stance on not wanting them hasn't changed."

"But why don't you?"

"Because, Angelo, I've grown up a Greek girl, told I should have babies from the time I was given my first baby doll. I want to break the pattern of the Greek-woman-as-breeder routine, okay? Now, let's talk about something else."

Angelo went quiet for a moment, watching birds in an arrow formation overhead, the flock suddenly dispersing toward the trees as if startled by a noise unheard to him. "I'm going to grab another beer. Want one?"

Phaedra shook her head.

Angelo scolded himself for downing that last brew. While washing his hands at the bathroom sink, down the hall he heard voices join in tune. It seemed sacrilege to miss someone's birthday song even if that someone was only one-year-old. He emerged in time to contribute to that final, drawn-out note, doing so from the kitchen doorway. The room was dark save for the candlelight, and from his seat at the counter little Yianni's round face resembled a jack-o-lantern in the dimness—shadows masking his eyes, his mouth a horizontal half-moon seemingly lit from within given its proximity to the tiny flame. He blew it out in a single attempt, everyone applauding the strength of his lungs until they threatened to unleash a powerful cry on account of the sudden blackness. A flick of a switch and the room brightened again, the baby gazing around happy-faced.

Adult-sized slices of cake made their rounds. Angelo enjoyed his piece beneath the glow of the heat lamps out near the bounce castle cavorting with new fervor as the structure itself seemed in a festive mood. In reality, of course, the increased vigor of the playhouse's tremors could be attributed to its inhabitants hopped up on sugar. One little boy in a Cookie Monster T-shirt came wobbling down the drawbridge and promptly threw up on the lawn while his parents, friends of Courtney, rushed over to comfort him and clean up the mess. Courtney insisted on handling it. Angelo had yet to speak at length with Courtney—Mike's on-again, off-again girlfriend and the mother of his child—but she seemed vaguely overwhelmed at the moment.

Angelo closed his eyes and took a bite of cake, guessing the mess would be cleaned when he opened them again. Perhaps Angelo wasn't in such a rush to have children after all.

He felt a hand on the small of his back. Phaedra had walked up in stealth, and despite the awkward end of their last interaction, she offered a soft touch and a genuine smile.

"Enjoying the cake?"

Angelo nodded around another mouthful.

Phaedra took a bite of her own slice. "So, how about we make a deal? Let's just say that at some point, a year or two from now, maybe three, I decide we can have a kid . . ."

"Well, speaking of, I was actually thinking—"

"I decide we can have a kid," Phaedra cut back in, "if you agree to finally move in with me and get a nine-to-five. Doesn't that seem fair?"

Angelo couldn't help but make a face. Phaedra's suggestion that they move in together wasn't all that shocking given that she had been hinting at it for the past six months. Never, though, had she mentioned wanting Angelo to flip corporate. Now, after getting to know this group of Greeks, a majority of whom were artistically inclined, the idea seemed somewhat preposterous. "I'm all for doing my part as a man to help support an eventual family, but I can't see myself taking a desk job."

"Fine. As long as you don't take a half-way gig."

"I thought you wanted me to focus on my art."

"Yeah, well, your child won't be able to eat your drawings!"

"Jesus, Phaedra! I don't know why you're taking this all so seriously! It's not like I've been pestering you for weeks about kids. Lots of women would be glad to hear their man bring up the idea. Maybe I should find a woman like that." Angelo's cheeks flushed with regret.

Phaedra didn't immediately reply, but the look on her face shouted exactly what Angelo wouldn't have been able to hear: *Why don't you, then?* "Listen, Angelo," she snapped at last, "I don't want kids, okay? No real reason, I just don't have that motherly urge! Got it?" Without waiting for a reply, she stalked off toward the house. The wake of her absence felt like those moments following an earthquake when beneath the fragile air drifts a current palpable in its strength; brimming with the promise of another jolt.

As guests armed with paper plates lined up in front of the grill, the savory food—burgers and dogs for the children, ribs and cobbed corn for adults— was served after the cake. Sensing Angelo's perplexion, Courtney explained, "The weird backward routine will become familiar when you have your own kids. Gotta bait the little ones with dessert first so that they stop begging and fighting for it, and then, after the sugar crash, you bring out the real meal."

Pete Saropoulos, first to return to the original picnic table, put down his stacked barbecue platter, licked his fingers, and then pulled up a seat beside Angelo. Once the entire crew had claimed their chairs, he presented Angelo with a sketch of a man in a pin-striped business suit holding a briefcase in one hand and a broken paintbrush in the other. Despite the graffiti-style exaggerated features, Angelo caught a resemblance between himself and the figure in the drawing.

"I present you with a futuristic vision of fatherhood."

Angelo couldn't help but chuckle, wondering if Pete overheard the discussion with Phaedra.

Pete gestured toward a group of fathers watching the bounce house, still rocking in spite of its last two casualties. "I think that's the same intensity I have when I'm staring at one of my canvases. Don't know about you, but I doubt my eyes could split that kind of focus between two creations, one artistic, the other biological."

Angelo took a breath, realizing that in his recent visions of fatherhood, all he ever imagined was a child. He always saw himself from behind as if he were ever to turn around there might not be a face.

Plates cleared and bellies full, everyone converged back in the house, claiming spots among the living room sofa, lounge chairs, and the carpet. The time had come to open gifts. Little Yianni stood in the middle of the floor, rotating a clumsy circle as though to show off his fresh diaper. He was gradually bestowed with presents when guests placed boxes at his feet as if in offering to some baby messiah.

Yianni tore into his bounty, regarding it the same bemused expression he had worn when in need of his last diaper change. Someone even gifted him a onesie made to resemble a tiny business suit, pinstripes and all.

Angelo was hit with another flash of Pete's sketch, unable to prevent himself from sinking into future visions of being trapped in a similar outfit, armed with a briefcase. Watching Mike kneel down and hold the little jumpsuit to his son's chest, Angelo couldn't help wanting to save the kid, and himself, from the corporate life being subconsciously imposed on them.

Another child, a boy of two or three, ran right over and toppled Yianni in an effort to get at one of the toys. Yianni popped back up unphased. However, the other boy's mother, a sandy-haired woman, yanked her son away before whacking him across the cheek with an open palm. As the child broke into wailing hysterics, everyone froze and exchanged stunned glances before lasering attention on the slap-happy mother. The scrutiny sent her skittering down the hallway while dragging her son behind. Only then did Yianni start to cry. The new sound seemed to snap everyone free of their unified shock.

Courtney gathered Yianni in her arms, then motioned for Mike to go check on the other mother and son. She paced with Yianni in her arms, cradling him against her shoulder, but he kept crying. "Phaedra," Courtney said, "can you hold him for a sec while I heat up a bottle?"

Phaedra's cheeks flushed at the request. She stepped back, as she had upon first arriving at the party when that little girl marched up to greet her. Courtney, meanwhile, oblivious to Phaedra's discomfort, took another step forward.

In their year together, Angelo had never once seen Phaedra hold anyone's kid. Then the unimaginable: Phaedra opened her arms toward the crying child. Upon receiving him, she didn't look so out of place. In the wake of his mother's departure, Yianni cried harder. Panic flashed over Phaedra's face, but then she brought the baby to her chest, rocked him gently up and down.

A round-faced woman made a tentative approach. "Do you want me to take him? I live in the brown house two doors down. He's used to me."

Phaedra continued to rock the baby. "No, thank you. I'm handling it."

Then, Yianni stopped crying. Phaedra met Angelo's eyes again, holding his gaze this time, and displaying an undeniable smile.

"Looking a little pale there. Everything cool?"

Angelo turned to find Mike Lagounis beside him. "I think I'm okay, man." Then, leaning in close and hushing his voice, he added, "So weird what happened earlier, right? The one mom whacking her kid like that."

"Lisa is one of Courtney's work friends," Mike whispered, "an overwhelmed single mother who drinks a little too hard. She was crying in there," he said, gesturing down the hall, "totally embarrassed and apologetic, really trying to make it up to her kid."

Angelo shrugged. "I don't judge. Hey, congrats again on this whole parent thing. You're doing great."

"Thank you, kind sir. Anyway, let's enjoy ourselves, huh? You're definitely part of the *parea* now, and it's time we grown-ups had our fun."

From his place at the round table nearest the screen door, Angelo watched the bounce house slowly sag and shrivel beneath the setting sun—a once mighty fortress reduced to a plastic puddle. All around the yard, kids lay napping atop blankets or quietly lounging in the grass, their energy sapped in time with the outflow of air from their fort. Conversely, the adults seemed to be revived by the dwindling structure as though they had sacked it in hopes of reclaiming the kingdom.

In the new darkness, Angelo reached into his back pocket and found Pete's sketch of the pin-striped "business man." He considered crumpling it, but instead retreated into the house, snagged a pencil, and took a seat at the kitchen table. He erased the stripes on the suit, added a flower to the lapel. Then, he replaced the briefcase with a drawing pad. Back outside, he found Pete hovering beneath one of the lamps. Angelo offered the sketch. "I tailored the suit."

Pete chuckled. "Business casual?"

Angelo's face turned pensive. "Nothing casual about the art business, brother."

The sky, fully dark now, small bulbs strung along the fence line flickered to life like nocturnal eyes blinking awake. Phaedra and Courtney stood in a corner, voices lilting happy notes on the breeze, though the content of their chatter was lost amid the airy pop music emanating from inside the house. When Courtney excused herself to retrieve something from inside, Angelo made his approach.

"Hey, there," Phaedra said.

Angelo gently took her hand. Hey. I'm sorry."

"Apology accepted," Phaedra said with a smile. "I shouldn't have hit you with an ultimatum like that. I think we have a lot of room to figure things out and make compromises when we need to."

"And I shouldn't have made that comment about finding someone else, because that's not what I want. I love you . . . kids or not."

Phaedra squeezed Angelo's hand, and then gestured toward the flattened play structure. "Guess the party's over, huh?"

"All good things come to an end, eventually."

"How do you mean?"

Angelo shrugged. "Just as it applies to parties and good times." He felt Phaedra's hand on the small of his back now. "Baby, I want what you want. I want what makes you happy."

"We both deserve to be happy together," Phaedra began. "I don't want kids, but I can't lose you."

Angelo experienced a sudden shortness of breath, a heaviness in his lungs. The sensation passed, though his apprehension didn't. "We can keep talking about all this."

"Yes."

"But not tonight. I'm through socializing, I've had enough of being around kids. Let's go home and crash in front of a movie. How's that sound?"

Phaedra didn't answer, but Angelo felt her move closer to him. That was all the response he needed.

town
triumph

One Sunday, Alex Kouros joined the Lake Merritt drum circle, that long-standing and loosely orchestrated assemblage of beat makers found beneath the arched pavilion on Sunday afternoons. The multiethnic percussionists, like quilted patchwork in their range of skin tones and vibrant clothing, thumped their drums to send vibrations cascading off the surrounding apartment buildings.

Amid the crowd of fellow onlookers, Alex smiled at a young black woman in a yellow sundress and matching headwrap. "Hey there."

"Hi," the woman said. Her amber eyes seemed well-paired with the honey inflection of her voice. She gestured to the stack of neon papers under Alex's arm. "Whatcha got?"

Alex's smile widened as he handed her one of the fliers featuring an illustration of an enormous oak tree with roots strangled by a network of computer cables. Above the image, the heading read, ARTLAND TRIBUNE. "My art fest is coming up next week. You should totally..."

A rumbling stampede silenced Alex. He followed the woman's furrow-browed gaze over the grassy slope to an ambush of twenty-first century pirates. Brandishing their loaded laptop bags like shoulder-slung weaponry, the techies would not be denied. Yelling threats that echoed the sentiments on their hoisted signs: KEEP THE MUSIC DOWN, OR ELSE!; STOP DISTURBING THE PEACE!; WE'RE MUTING YOU!, the invaders pillaged the scene. They stomped between the green, orange, and blue picnic blankets of families frozen in shock.

Alex pushed his way toward the middle of the fray. In grasping the arm of one protestor, he nearly spun the man full around. "What the hell are you guys doing?"

The techie scowled, jutting a finger toward the rise of new condos across the way. "Isn't it obvious you're too close to our homes? We demand to see permits! This is an illegal gathering!"

Alex let go of the man's arm, if only to refrain from shoving him to the ground. "Hey, asshole, how about a permit for your right to gentrify?"

Another techie, a beefier version of the first, came to his friend's aid. "What's the problem here?"

"*You!*" fumed Alex. "Now, look around, do you see any mics?"

In unison, the techies blinked and gawked.

"Exactly," Alex said. "City policy says musicians can play as long as they don't have an amplified sound system." Then, with a smile, he added, "If you were from Oakland, you'd know that."

Pedaling up in spandex shorts were a trio of pink-thighed bike cops, their eyes hidden behind identical mirrored shades. Gesturing toward Alex, a young blonde officer asked, "This guy bothering you folks?"

Despite the springtime breeze, sweat beaded Alex's forehead as pleaded his case. "I grew here! I was just explaining the lay of the land. Artists don't need permission to perform . . ."

One of the other cops, silver moustache and drooping jowls, stepped in front of the younger officer to address the techies. "Friends, I'm afraid this young man is correct. These drummers have been here a lot longer than you, and they'll be here long after you've moved on."

Despite the techies stomping in protest like toddlers amid tantrums, the bike cops pedaled away. But Alex's satisfaction was short-lived.

At his car, he found another note stuck to his driver side window. From his glove compartment he gathered a mound of hostile Stick-Its to which he added the newest reading I'M WATCHING YOU. Then, he crossed the street to confront the glass and steel monolith that had seemed to appear one day, like similar structures throughout the city, fully assembled as a newly landed alien vessel from planet Gentrification. On occasion he had witnessed an emergence of extraterrestrial life: men and women in business casual rather than space gear, though they were spaced-out just the same. Among them, Alex had once or twice spotted his food truck's mysterious visitor, Mr. Odezmir. But right then, as he glanced to his left and right, he saw no sign of the man.

While driving to a rehearsal party for the upcoming festivities, Alex succumbed to a familiar reverie. If not via the highest mountain top, then from one of the tallest buildings Alex's grandest art fest, ARTLAND TRIBUNE, would transmit citywide, brighter and bolder than anything he had attempted before. In his recurring daydream, from street level he gazed up through binoculars to where his friend Daphne stood on a ledge at the peak of the Oakland Tribune tower, right next to the giant clock with its numbers glowing ruddy against the purplish blush of twilight. Her dark hair thrashed in the wind like palm fronds in a hurricane. Her voice projected directly into the gust so that her stanzas, amplified through a powerful, physics-defying megaphone, were sent throughout the Town like newly released birds.

"*This bayside port of call is scrap metal behind cyclone fence. Town of discard. Tribune Tower infamous, auto bodies old school voluptuous. Brick long standing forlorn in sister city shadow . . ."*

After losing himself yet again to the same daydream, Alex blinked back to reality. He sat among friends in the backyard of the East Oakland residence belonging to his homegirl, and aspiring novelist, Jane Trueblood. Standing on a milk crate beneath a pair of apple trees, Daphne read her poem as part of this rehearsal for the Artland fest.

"Yes, we too arrived here from somewhere else, but way before it was a destination on your rideshare map . . ."

Daphne's clever turns of phrase inspired finger snaps and murmurs of encouragement from her wide-ranging audience consisting of both well-tailored OG's clouded in Black & Mild smoke, and pierced pubescents with half-moon hoop earrings. Alex nodded at Darnell Dawkins seated a few folding chairs over with his cherished trumpet.

Daphne earned applause upon finishing, and Jane's blue-gray pitbull, Tweety, with tail wagging, escorted her back to her chair. Alex's enthusiasm soared at the thought of Daphne reading the same piece at his Artland festival. After refilling his red Solo cup from a nearby keg, he ambled over to the card table where Jane had set down a platter of Navajo tacos, the fluffy fry bread glistening golden against the porcelain plate.

"So you never gave me a definite answer," Alex said, sipping his IPA.

Jane fingered her silver necklace with the turquoise feather charm, the jewelry she called her "Indian trading post piece." So many white people fawned over it that she had relayed to Alex a temptation to, in explaining the accessory's origin, come up with a sad, "reservation story." "I told you I'm already booked that day. I'm reading at David's event over in Berkeley, but it starts at four so there's a chance I can still make your Artland fest."

"Fair enough. Now, let me ask you this," Alex continued, showing Jane the latest sticky note, "What would you do if every time you walked out to your car someone had left a complaint note about noise, or the way you parked, or your existence in general."

"I'd remind myself that it's just life in 'New Oakland.'"

Alex listened to the surrounding chatter backdropped by understated notes zig-zagging from Darnell's horn as he now sat near the fence gently blowing into his trumpet. Alex crossed the yard and took a seat next to him.

"What it is, Greek? You philosophizing over there?"

"Something like that. How you holding up these days?"

Darnell leaned back, the horn in his lap shimmering like the herringbone chain that had been his trademark in eleventh grade. "If she loved me like she said she did, she'll come around. I told her, take as long as you need to work on yourself, get your shit straight, and maybe I'll see you then. Best way to play it, seems like. Can't get too lonely when I've got my music."

Alex smiled again. "So, you'll play at Artland, right?"

Darnell winced. "Well about that, Greek, I'm grateful for the offer, and I was really looking forward to it—"

"No excuses, friend. If you can't do it, I understand. But why don't you at least come and check it out? Who knows, might find yourself so inspired that you decide to get on stage after all. A pair of songs, what's that, ten minutes max? I bet you can spare ten minutes. What better way to spend six-hundred seconds?"

"Shit, Alex, you're *good*. How can I say no to that pitch?"

Alex spread his palms. "What? It was only a suggestion."

"Yeah, right. I'm down, but I'll have to cut early to be back at the job the next morning."

"Since when do you work construction on weekends?"

"Since Oakland became the new hot spot. All these folks moving in, we can't put up condos and apartment complexes fast enough. Shit, that big office building right across from the bar where you're doing your art thing, we put that up only about six months ago. Now we're working on another spot not far from there. I'll tell you, man, these days I'm spending more time drivin' that damn crane than I am my own car. "

"I believe it," said Alex. "How's it feel to be building homes none of us locals can afford?"

Darnell sighed. "If I could do the job with my eyes closed, I damn sure would."

The Friday before the Artland fest, Alex arrived at Frank Ogawa plaza for a final pre-festival check of the site. His green Artland pennant lay torn and tangled among the tree branches. With a nagging anger in his chest, Alex glanced around for any trace of the culprits. From the shadows of the plaza's landmark oak tree, emerged a vaguely recognizable face . . . startling blue eyes, sharp cheekbones . . . the man named Mr. Odezmir who had visited the food truck and inflicted Alex with the evil eye.

This time, Alex was armed with the curse-warding blue eye charm necklace fresh from the repair shop. With squared shoulders and chest puffed, he confronted his mysterious adversary. "What's the deal? Why'd you rip my banner?"

Mr. Odezmir narrowed his gaze. "It clashes with the advertisements for our yoga concert. You can't hold your event here."

"Says who? If I remember right, you didn't have a problem with where we parked our food truck with all your gushing about our gyros."

With a raised arm and a smug glance, the man held up a city permit. "We've got new plans for the plaza, and Oakland, *new* Oakland, is behind us."

Turning his back on his rival, Alex's heart went the way of the dusk sun; searing in its surrender to the day's close.

The sensation so unfamiliar, Alex couldn't identify—or admit—the source behind his pounding heart until its rapid beat nearly overwhelmed him. *Panic.* It worsened with each ring that went unanswered. When Pete's voice finally sounded on the other line, Alex didn't waste time. "Bro, what took you so long to pick up! Meet me at Jumping Acorn!"

"You mean Sustenance? What are you—"

"Man, how stupid could I be? Why didn't I just get the damn permit!"

"Hold up, what—"

"Never mind! Just meet me at the spot. Now!"

Despite it having been open for quite some time, Alex was still taken aback by the sight of the fancy eatery named 'SUSTENANCE'. The team of burly security guards, and the constantly circling patrol cars, were no doubt a response to the restaurant's big, shiny window being broken months earlier. Alex turned away from the glass to see Pete Saropoulos approaching, his sneakers gleaming like chrome in the warm glow emanating from the restaurant's interior.

"Cool kicks," said Alex.

"Ah, yeah. They used to be white. I was working on a new piece the other day, dribbled a few splotches of silver, and then said the hell with it, I might as well paint the damn—hey, you're not even listening!"

Alex pointed to the restaurant window. "Go figure, this is their hangout." Beyond the glass, with tattooed stars twinkling the length of their forearms, a crowd of women sat opposite men with unironic handlebar moustaches. "I recognize them from the other day," added Alex.

"Who?"

Alex sighed. "The Gentrify Gang."

Pete raised an eyebrow.

"I don't know what else to call them; bunch of assholes who stormed the drum circle. Their leader, Odezmir, tore up my festival banner. Damn, I was stupid enough to not get a permit for Artland!"

"Man," started Pete, "I say 'fuck a piece of paper,' just like you said 'fuck the sticky notes.' Let's gather the whole crew," said Pete. "Power in numbers. Red tape be damned, bro, we're going to put on this festival!"

Some of the customary brightness returned to Alex's face. "Now you're talking."

On a bright Saturday, the afternoon of ARTLAND TRIBUNE, Alex rallied his troops—Angelo, Pete, Johnny, Mike, Daphne, and Courtney—at Frank Ogawa Plaza. "You all ready? Picture the three-hundred Spartans marching against an opposing army that's threatening to conquer Ancient Greece and the rest of the world along with it. Now, picture us as the modern Spartans, the *Oakland* Spartans, braced for battle."

Johnny paused in his singing to chuckle. "Dude, can you give that a second take, only a little more melodramatic this time?"

"Joke all you want," said Alex, "but the show is going on as scheduled, and we might just have a fight on our hands. I want us all prepared for battle. Not with our fists, but with our talents."

"Come again?" said Angelo.

"The gentrifiers want to defeat us," Alex went on, "but, remember, we grew here! The roots are too deep to cut down. Johnny, you're going to sing like you've never sung! Angelo, come armed with your newest masterpiece! Pete, bring all the colors in your paint palette! Phaedra, you're the practical one, make sure we stay focused! Daphne, it's poetry time! Courtney, hold the babies extra tight, because kids . . . *Oakland* kids . . . are the future!"

Then, as if propelled by the momentum of Alex's speech, the group rallied forth with shouts of "The show must go on!"

Alex stood at the fringes of Frank Ogawa Plaza, backed by his entire crew. Across the way, in the center of the square, that gang of gentrifiers headed by the evil-eyed Mr. Odezmir. Beyond them, the stage. It appeared as if the Gentrifiers were daring his group to cross over enemy lines. Meanwhile, in anticipation of a brawl, there gathered a great crowd: hipsters in red-and-black lumberjack shirts alongside young locals with their slouched stances resonating classic Oakland cool.

Alex, bolstered by the company of his troops, squared his stance. "You've been watching us from the beginning. Just like Missus Mavromatis told me." He fingered his protective medallion.

"You could put it that way," said Odezmir.

"This fest is about building community, you realize that?"

Odezmir shrugged again. "I've witnessed your previous disasters."

From his place in front of the Plaza's main platform, Alex felt the crowd edging near, murmurs of impatience in the wind. He dared a step forward, and one of the Gentrifiers pushed him back. But when he and the crew took a collective step, the Gentrifiers retreated. Right then, it came to Alex: Art was the revolution, and there was no denying it. He jogged up the platform steps and returned to the main grounds with mic in hand. "Thanks for coming out today, folks. Change of plans. We're bringing the art to the street." He marched toward the Plaza's edge, and beyond its perimeter the greater city beckoned.

Pete was first to follow Alex's example. Alone he graced the stage and retrieved his painting, bringing it down into the crowd. Angelo was next with his canvas, then Johnny and Daphne with the remaining microphones. They trailed Alex into the street, followed by the wave of spectators.

Before long, Odezmir and his Gentrifiers, alone in front of the stage, glanced to-and-fro in confusion; the line blurred between audience and performer, between art and life. There was no use for the Gentrifiers to defend the plaza since "Artland" borders had spread beyond it. Soon even the barriers separating local and transplant diminished until nothing remained except music and paint and poetry and prose—homegrown, here to stay.

Through the line of trees, like a swarm of wasps, walkie-talkies buzzing, the bike cops descended on the scene.

reading guide

Theme: **IDENTITY**

From the book's beginning, the theme of identity is recurrent in *We Grew Here*. How do our job choices, talents, and birthplaces shape our identities? Are identities stable parts of us or do they change over time and circumstance?

Prompt:

Think of a time when you were searching for identity whether through career, culture, or social circle. List a series of feelings you experienced during that period. Using your list, create a story or poem that explores the challenges and rewards of claiming an identity.

Representative Stories:

- "Shades of Other" (p. 63)
- "Invisible Friends" (p. 71)
- "Earth Tones" (p. 153)

Theme: **HOME**

We Grew Here is essentially about home; how we claim, define, and create it. Many of the characters who are fiercely loyal to their hometown of Oakland also pledge allegiance to Greece as their ancestral home. Some do so while looking down on Oakland's transplant communities. Can one claim multiple homes as their own? Do we hold a certain ownership over our birthplaces? If so, how? If not, why?

Prompt:

Think of a time when you were searching for identity whether through career, culture, or social circle. List a series of feelings you experienced during that period. Using your list, create a story or poem that explores the challenges and rewards of claiming an identity.

Representative Stories:

- "Broken Glass" (p. 112)
- "We Grew Here" (p. 130)

Theme: **JUSTICE**

We Grew Here explores various timely social issues in portraying Oakland's historic spirit of activism. As works of art, do novels, movies, and albums have a responsibility to address societal concerns? Why or why not? What are the risks and rewards an artist takes in embracing a certain social cause?

Prompt:

Choose one of the stories in *We Grew Here* and identify the main social issue it explores. Once identified, write a poem exploring your stance on this same issue.

Representative Stories:

- "Earth Tones" (p. 153)
- "Sacrificial Lamb" (p. 168)

Theme: **GENTRIFICATION**

Another major theme in *We Grew Here* is gentrification, the act of wealthy/privileged people moving into poorer urban areas and renovating housing, thereby attracting new businesses and raising the cost of living often at the expense of long-time residents.

For instance, in the "Mati" story Ms. Mavromatis is rumored to have "cast a spell" on her disrespectful, transplant neighbors, ultimately forcing them to leave the neighborhood. In what other ways do the novel's characters combat gentrification in Oakland? Are some characters more accepting of the trend than others? How so?

Prompt:

Create a list of gentrification's pro's and con's, three to five examples under each category. Next, write a short essay, 300 to 500 words illustrating your ideas as to how gentrification can or cannot be made more harmonious for old and new residents alike.

Representative Stories:

- "Jumping Acorn" (p. 12)
- "Mati" (p. 52)
- "We Grew Here" (p. 130)

Theme: **ART AS LIFE**

Oakland reference (art culture/history) here A majority of the characters in We Grew Here have chosen to pursue a life in the arts at all costs, often sacrificing security and livelihood.

Alex, for instance, chases the "ultimate hustle" as a way to avoid the corporate world and cement a place for himself amid Oakland's art community. How does this pursuit strengthen or challenge his relationships? In what ways do his values align with or stray from his Greek culture? How do his Oakland roots influence this hustler's mentality?

Prompt:

Think about the pursuit of your dreams, whether artistic or otherwise. What obstacles have you encountered? Have your friends, family, and romantic partners helped or hindered you? Using the term "ultimate hustle" create a poem illustrating your quest to reach your goals. Perhaps highlight your favorite phrases in one or more sections in the novel, and incorporate certain lines into your own poem.

Representative Stories:

- "Kissing Booth" (p. 3)
- "Heroes with Gyros" (p. 28)
- "High Note" (p. 104)
- "Nine-to-Five" (p. 119)

acknowledgments

Mama; the first artist to inspire me, how I know you're smiling from above. Before you got sick, I voiced my frustrations and doubts about the writing biz. You wouldn't let me get discouraged. Now this book has found a home! Your support and love is/was always fierce! Love you in heaven!

Much love to all my family in Oakland, the wider Bay, and in Greece … Dad, you are the original storyteller; thank you for instilling in me a love of our culture and history.

To the Oakland Greek community; *agape se olous!* Among you I will always have a home.

To my dear friend and mentor, Oakland's own, author Jess Mowry, thank you for the faith!

And, of course, much gratitude to the Nomadic Press family! J.K. Fowler, I immensely thank you for believing in this book; from the beginning I felt Nomadic was the perfect fit! To Nina Sacco, my fantastic, fantastic editor, working with you has truly been a pleasure! I so appreciate your keen insight and sharp skill. Together, we took this novel to the next level.

Prior publishing credits:
"Jumping Acorn" originally appeared in *Oakland Review,* issue 4.

Apollo Papafrangou

Hailing from Oakland, California, Apollo Papafrangou is the author of the acclaimed debut novel *Wings of Wax* (Olive Leaf Editions, 2016). He has also written for HBO Films, which optioned the film rights to his story *The Fence* (2000-2004). His fiction and poetry has appeared in *ZYZZYVA* magazine, *Oakland Review*, *The Bookends Review*, *Sparkle & Blink*, and the Simon & Schuster anthology *Trapped*. He holds an MFA in Creative Writing from Mills College.

OTHER WAYS TO SUPPORT NOMADIC PRESS' WRITERS

In 2020, two funds geared specifically toward supporting our writers were created: the **Nomadic Press Black Writers Fund** and the **Nomadic Press Emergency Fund**.

The former is a forever fund that puts money directly into the pockets of our Black writers. The latter provides dignity-centered emergency grants to any of our writers in need.

Please consider supporting these funds. You can also more generally support Nomadic Press by donating to our general fund via nomadicpress.org/donate and by continuing to buy our books. As always, thank you for your support!

Scan below for more information and/or to donate.
You can also donate at nomadicpress.org/store.